The
Amelia
Jane
Collection

By Enid Blyton

Naughty Amelia Jane
Amelia Jane Is Naughty Again
Amelia Jane Gets Into Trouble
Amelia Jane Again
Good Idea, Amelia Jane

The Adventures of the Wishing-Chair
The Wishing-Chair Again
More Wishing-Chair Stories
The Wishing-Chair Collection

The Enchanted Wood
The Magic Faraway Tree
The Folk of the Faraway Tree
Up the Faraway Tree
The Magic Faraway Tree Collection

The Caravan Family
The Seaside Family
The Buttercup Farm Family
The Queen Elizabeth Family
Are We There Yet?

The Amelia Jane Collection

Enid Blyton

EGMONT

EGMONT

We bring stories to life

First published in Great Britain 1946 by Newnes
This edition published in 2019 by Egmont UK Limited
The Yellow Building, 1 Nicholas Road, London W11 4AN

Enid Blyton ®, The Magic Faraway Tree ®
and Enid Blyton's signature are registered trade marks of
Hodder & Stoughton Limited
Text © 1946 Hodder & Stoughton Limited
Illustrations © 2019 Hodder & Stoughton Limited
Interior illustrations by Erin Brown

ISBN 978 1 4052 9401 0

www.egmont.co.uk

A CIP catalogue record for this title is available from the British Library

Printed and bound in Great Britain by the CPI Group

54023/001

MIX
Paper from
responsible sources
FSC® C020471

Contents

Naughty
Amelia
Jane

Contents

Naughty Amelia Jane

The toys in the nursery were very friendly with the small pixies who lived in the bushes below the nursery window. The pixies had no wings, but they managed to climb up the tall pear tree and get in at the window whenever it was open. So you can guess that the toys and the pixies had many a good game!

There was one very naughty toy, who often made the others really angry. This was Amelia Jane, a big, long-legged doll with an ugly face, a bright red frock, and yellow hair. She hadn't come from a shop, like the others, but had been made at home. Shop-toys nearly always have good manners, and know how to behave themselves – but Amelia Jane, not being a shop-toy, had no manners at all, and didn't care what she said or did!

Once she poured a jug of milk down Tom the toy soldier's neck, and that made him wet and uncomfortable for two days. Another time she threw a woollen ball up so high that it went into the goldfish globe, and made the poor goldfish jump almost out of his skin. Then, when the teddy bear climbed up to get the ball out of the water, Amelia Jane climbed up behind him, gave him a push – and there was the poor bear, spluttering away in the water, and trying his hardest to swim, whilst the goldfish darted at him in fury.

Dear dear, how Amelia Jane laughed, and how all the other toys shouted at her!

Whatever would she do next?

The next thing she did was to catch a bee
in a matchbox, and then, when the sailor doll
needed matches, she gave him the matchbox,
pretending that there were matches inside.
You can imagine how scared he was when
a bee flew out and stung him on the nose!

'Amelia Jane, you are a perfect nuisance,' said the toys angrily. 'Can't you settle down and be good like us? One day you will do something that will get us all into trouble!'

'Pooh!' said Amelia Jane rudely. 'I shan't!'

But she did do something very naughty indeed the next time.

She was hunting about in Nanny's work-basket for a thimble to play with, when she came across Nanny's scissors. Ho! Now she could have a fine game of cutting!

So she took the scissors and began to snip-snip-snip everything! The other toys were sitting in a corner playing a game of snap, and they didn't notice at first what Amelia Jane was doing. They wouldn't let Amelia play snap with them because she said 'Snap!' when it wasn't, and took away all their cards.

So Amelia Jane had a lovely time all by herself. She snipped a hole in the curtains, and then she snipped another! Then she went to the hearth-rug and cut a whole corner off that! Then she found Nanny's handkerchief on the floor, and do you know, she cut it into twenty-two tiny pieces! It was one of Nanny's best hankies too, with a pretty lace edge. But Amelia Jane didn't care about that!

Then she went to the carpet and began to snip little bits of it here and there. The carpet was a green one with red roses, and wherever Amelia could see a rose, she snipped! Wasn't it dreadful of her?

The toys took no notice. They were having such a lovely game. Amelia grew cross with them for being happy without her. So what do you suppose she did?

She went up behind the pink rabbit and snipped his tail off!

Goodness! You should have seen how he jumped!

'Oooooooh!' he yelled. 'She's snipped my tail off! Look! Oh, the wicked, wicked doll!'

'And look what else she's done!' cried the toys in horror, pointing to the spoilt hanky, the snipped rug, and the cut carpet. 'And look, she's spoilt the curtains too. Oh, what trouble we shall get into! Nanny will know it must be the toys, and she will throw us all into the dustbin! Oh!'

The toys stared in horror at all that the naughty doll had done. The pink rabbit cried bitterly, for he felt dreadful without a tail. Oh dear! How he would be laughed at, now that he hadn't a tail! Tom the toy soldier put his arm round him and comforted him.

'Don't worry, Bunny,' he said. 'We shall all love you just the same, even if you don't wear a tail, and look rather like a guinea-pig!'

The pink rabbit cried all the more loudly when he heard that. 'I don't want to be like a guinea-pig!' he wept. 'I want to be like a rabbit! I hate Amelia Jane! Punish her, Tom! She is a very wicked doll!'

Amelia Jane laughed. She loved doing naughty things. She liked seeing all the toys staring in horror at the mischief she had done. Ha, Ha! That would teach them to play snap without her!

'Give me those scissors,' said Tom sternly.

'Shan't!' said Amelia Jane, twirling them round in her big hand.

'I said, "Give me those scissors!"' ordered

the toy soldier.

'I said "Shan't!"' said Amelia Jane, 'and if you talk to me like that, Tom, I'll chop your hat into little pieces! Then you'll look horrid!'

'You naughty, wicked doll!' said Tom, in a fury. But he didn't dare to try to take the scissors away, for they had very sharp points, and he really was afraid that Amelia Jane would cut up his lovely hat. He was very proud of it, and he didn't want anything to happen to it.

'Whatever shall we do?' said the teddy bear. The toys all looked at one another in despair.

Then they heard a little scraping noise at the window, and they saw their friends, the pixies, creeping in at the crack at the bottom.

'Hallo, Toys! You look very miserable!' said the pixies, scrambling down from the window-seat to the floor. 'What's the matter? Have you lost a pound and found a penny?'

'No,' said the toys. 'Just look here, pixies, at what Amelia Jane has done!'

'I say!' said the pixies, staring at all the damage. 'Why did you let her have scissors? And look, she still has them. You ought to take them away from her before she does any more mischief.'

'She won't let us have them,' said Tom. 'She says she will chop my hat into little pieces if I try to take them from her.'

'Oho, we'll soon see to that!' said the biggest pixie at once. 'Scissors, come to me!'

He waved his little gold wand – and immediately the scissors flew out of Amelia Jane's hand and went to the pixie. He caught them and gave them to Tom.

'Oh, thank you,' said the toys gratefully. 'I suppose you couldn't help us to mend all these dreadful holes and slits that Amelia has made?'

'Oh yes, I think so,' said the biggest pixie. 'We'll just go and get our needles and thread, and come back to help you. We'll sew everything so that you won't see even a tiny stitch! We are very clever at stitching, you know. Once we sewed all the petals on a daisy that had lost hers in a rainstorm – and you really couldn't see that they were not growing! As for that handkerchief, we'll use a bit of magic for that, and all the bits will join together so that Nanny will never know it has been cut!'

The pixies fetched their needles and thread, and soon they were sitting on the carpet and on the rug, mending all the slits and cuts, and two of them mended the curtains. Then the biggest pixie put a spell into his needle and sewed on the bunny's tail again. It didn't hurt a bit because of the spell.

The bunny was so grateful.

The handkerchief was mended too – and everything was put right.

'There!' said the pixies, in delight. 'We've done all we can!'

'We can't thank you enough!' said the toys. 'You may be sure that if ever we can help you in return we will!'

'As for Amelia Jane,' said the biggest pixie, 'I should keep her a prisoner in the toy-cupboard until she says she is sorry and won't be naughty any more. Here is a spell that will keep her there!'

Tom took the spell. It was in a little box, and when it was taken out and blown over Amelia, she had to stay where she was put. The toys surrounded the naughty doll, pushed her into the cupboard, and then blew the spell at her.

She couldn't move her legs! There she had to stay!

At first she was very angry. Then she was frightened, and begged to be set free. She saw the toys going happily about their play, and she wanted to join them. It was dreadfully dull in the toy-cupboard all alone except for a box of bricks that never said a word.

'I'm sorry, Toys! Do set me free!' begged Amelia Jane. 'I will try very hard not to be naughty any more.'

'If we could be sure you would do good things and not naughty ones, we *would* set you free,' said Tom. 'But we don't trust you. You have never done a good or brave thing all the time you have been with us.'

Amelia Jane was just going to answer him when there came a tapping at the window.

The toys looked up. A small red robin was there. He looked most excited.

'What is it?' shouted the toys, swarming up to the window-seat.

'It's the pixies!' said the robin. 'They have been attacked by the goblins! They have hidden in the old hollow tree, but the goblins are cutting it down! Can you rescue them?'

'How?' said Tom, upset and bothered to

hear such bad news.

'I don't know,' said the robin. 'You'll have to think of something – but hurry, because at any moment the goblins may get them!'

He flew off, and the toys crowded together, all talking at once.

'Toys, Toys, I have a plan!' cried Amelia Jane from the cupboard. 'Let me fly the toy aeroplane out of the window. It will frighten the goblins terribly, and they are sure to run away. Then, before they come back, the pixies can get into the aeroplane and I'll fly it safely back here!'

'All right!' shouted the toys, excited. 'It's a good idea. Set her free, Tom.'

So Amelia Jane was set free. The aeroplane was run up to her, and she got in. Rr-rr-rr-rr-rr! It shot up into the air and out of the window.

How exciting it was! Amelia was a bit afraid of falling out, but she managed to guide the aeroplane to the hollow tree. Then down she flew – and all the little goblins who were cutting down the tree to get at the pixies inside, cried out in horror:

'Run! Run! The aeroplane is coming down on top of us!'

They scattered in fright. Amelia stopped the aeroplane and landed by the hollow tree. She called to the pixies:

'Pixies! Quickly! Get into my aeroplane! I've come to rescue you!'

The pixies all shot out of the hollow tree at once and clambered into the plane. When the goblins saw what was happening they gave a shout of rage and ran to the aeroplane at once – but it was too late.

Rr-rr-rr-rr-rr!
It rose into the air, and
flew straight back to the
nursery window. In two minutes
the pixies were safe in the nursery
with the toys, and how pleased they were!

'Amelia Jane has turned over a new leaf,' said the pixies, in surprise. 'Brave Amelia Jane! Thank you so much for rescuing us!'

'Don't mention it!' said Amelia. 'I am trying very hard to be good now.'

And you will be pleased to hear that she certainly *was* good for a little while, but I'm afraid it didn't last for very long!

Amelia Jane Gets a Shock

Well, for a little while Amelia Jane was very good – and then, oh dear, she forgot all her promises, and became really naughty! The things she did!

She took a needle and cotton out of Nanny's work-basket, and sewed up the sleeves of the teddy bear's new coat when he wasn't looking. So when he went to put on his coat, he simply could *not* put his arms through the sleeves anyhow! He just couldn't find the way in – because the sleeves were sewn up! How Amelia Jane laughed to see him!

The next night she hid behind the curtain

and began to mew like a cat. The toys were not very fond of Tibs the cat, because he sometimes chewed them. So they all stopped playing and looked round to see where Tibs was.

'I can hear him mewing!' said the teddy bear. 'He must be behind the door.'

But he wasn't. Amelia mewed again. The toys hunted all about for the cat. They even looked in the coal-scuttle, and under the hearth-rug, which made Amelia laugh till she nearly choked! She mewed again, very loudly.

'Where is that cat!' cried Tom the toy soldier, in despair. 'We've looked everywhere! Is he behind the curtain?'

'No, there's only Amelia Jane there!' said the golden-haired doll, looking. 'There's no cat.'

Well, of course, they didn't find any cat at all! And Amelia Jane didn't tell them it was she who had been mewing, so to this day they wonder where Tibs hid himself that night!

Then Amelia Jane saw a soda-water siphon left in a corner of the room. She knew how it worked, because she had seen Nanny using one. Oh, what fun it would be to squirt all the toys! She stole towards it – picked it up, and dear me, it was heavy! She ran at the surprised Tom, pressed down the handle – and out gushed the soda-water all over him!

'Ow! Ooh!' he shouted, in astonishment. 'What is it? What is it? Amelia Jane, you ought to be ashamed of yourself!'

But she wasn't a bit ashamed. She was just enjoying herself thoroughly! She ran after the teddy bear and soaked him with soda-water too. She squirted lots over the clockwork mouse, and made him so wet that for two days his clockwork went wrong, and he couldn't be wound up. She squirted the pink rabbit, and he got into the wastepaper basket and couldn't get out, which worried him very much, because he was so afraid that Jane, the cleaner, would throw him away the next day! But she didn't, which was very lucky.

'Amelia Jane is up to her tricks again,' said the clockwork clown, frowning. 'We shall have no peace at all. What shall we do?'

'Take away her key!' said the clockwork mouse.

'She hasn't one, silly!' said Tom.

'Lock her in the cupboard!' said the teddy bear.

'She knows how to undo it from the inside,' said the pink rabbit gloomily.

Nobody spoke for a whole minute. They were all thinking hard.

Then the clockwork clown gave a little laugh. 'I know!' he said. 'I've thought of an idea. It's quite simple, but it might work.'

'What?' cried everyone.

'Let's polish Amelia Jane's shoes underneath and make them very, very slippery,' said the clown. 'Then, if she begins to run after us with soda-water siphons or things like that, down she'll go!'

'But she won't like that,' said the golden-haired doll, who was rather tender-hearted.

'Well, *we* don't like the tricks she plays on us!' said Tom. 'We'll do it, Clown! When she next takes her shoes off we'll polish them underneath till they are as slippery as glass!'

The very next night Amelia Jane took off her shoes because she said her feet were hot. She put the shoes into a corner and then danced round the nursery in her stockinged feet, enjoying herself. The clown picked up the shoes and ran away to the back of the toy-cupboard with them. He had a tiny duster there, and a little bit of polish he had taken out of Jane's polish jar when the nursery had been cleaned out. Aha, Amelia Jane, you'll be sorry for all your tricks!

The clown polished and rubbed, rubbed and polished. The soles of the shoes shone. They were as slippery as could be! The clown put them back and waited for Amelia Jane to put them on. This she very soon did, for she had stepped on a pin and pricked her foot!

As she put her shoes on, she thought out a naughty trick!

I'll run after all the toys with that pin I trod on! she thought. Oooh! That will make them rush away into all the corners! What fun it will be to frighten them!

She buttoned her shoes and took the nasty long pin into her hand. Then she stood up and looked round, her naughty eyes gleaming. I'll run after that fat little teddy bear! she thought. So off she went, straight at the teddy bear, holding the pin out in front of her.

'Amelia Jane, put that pin down!' shouted the teddy bear in fright – but before Amelia Jane had taken three steps, her very, very slippery shoes slid along the ground and down she fell, bumpity-bump! She *was* so surprised!

Up she got again and took a few more steps towards the teddy bear – but her shoes slipped and down she fell! Bumpity-bump! She hit her head on the fender!

'What's the matter with the carpet?' cried Amelia Jane in a rage. 'It keeps making me fall down!'

'Ha ha! ho ho!' laughed the toys. 'Perhaps there is slippery magic about, Amelia Jane!'

'Oh, I believe you toys have something to do with it!' shouted the angry doll. Up she got and took the pin in her hand again. 'I'll show you what happens to people who put slippery magic on the floor! Here comes my pin!'

She tried to run at Tom, who was laughing so much that the tears ran all down his face. But down she went again, bumpity-bump – and oh my, the pin stuck into her knee! Yes, it really did – she fell on it!

How Amelia Jane squealed! How Amelia Jane wept! 'Oh, the horrid pin! Oh, how it hurts!' she cried.

'Well, Amelia Jane, it serves you right,' said the pink rabbit. 'You were going to prick *us* with that pin and now it's pricked *you*! You know how it feels!'

Amelia Jane threw the pin away in a rage. The clown picked it up and flung it into the fire! He wasn't going to have pins about the nursery!

Amelia Jane got up again. 'I'm going to bandage my knee where the pin pricked it,' she said. She ran to the toy cupboard – but before she was halfway there, her slippery shoes slid away beneath her – and down she sat with a dreadful bumpity-bumpity-bump!

The toys laughed. Amelia Jane cried bitterly. The golden-haired doll felt sorry for her. 'Don't cry any more, Amelia Jane,' she said. 'Take your shoes off and you won't fall again. We played a trick on you – but you can't complain because you have so often tricked *us*! You should not play jokes on other people if you can't take a joke yourself!'

Amelia Jane took her shoes off. She saw how the clown had polished them underneath, and she went very red. She knew quite well she could not grumble if people were unkind – because she too had been unkind.

'I'll try and be good, Toys,' she said at last. 'It's difficult for me, because I'm not a shop-toy like you, so I haven't learnt good manners and nice ways. But I may be good one day!'

The toys thought it was nice of her to say all that. The golden-haired doll came to help her bandage her knee. The clown put a bandage round her head where she had bumped it. She looked so funny that they didn't know whether to laugh or cry at her.

Amelia Jane did enjoy being fussed! She was as nice as could be to the toys – but oh dear, oh dear, I do somehow feel perfectly certain that she can't be good for long!

Amelia Jane at the Sea

Once it happened that Amelia Jane, the big,
naughty doll, was taken down to the seaside
with some of the other toys. The clockwork
clown went, the brown teddy bear, Tom the
toy soldier, and the golden-haired doll. They
went in the car with the children, and they
were all most excited.

'I shall dig in the sand and throw it over
everybody!' said naughty Amelia Jane. 'And I
shall get my pail and fill it full of water and
pour it down Tom's neck! Ho, won't he
jump!'

'You'll do nothing of the sort, Amelia Jane,'
said Tom at once. 'You know how often

you've promised to be good. Well, just you remember your promise.'

'And I shall push the clockwork clown into a rock-pool and make him sit down there with all his clothes on,' said Amelia Jane, with a naughty giggle.

'You mustn't!' cried the clown, in alarm. 'If you do that, my clockwork will get rusty and I shan't wind up properly – then I won't be able to walk any more, or turn head-over-heels!'

The children often took the toys down to the beach with them. After dinner the children went to have a rest, and the toys were left in a sheltered corner of the beach. No one ever came there, so the children knew they were quite safe. And it was whilst the toys were left alone there that Amelia Jane behaved so very badly. She did all she said she would, and more too.

She threw sand all over the golden-haired doll, and it went into her eyes dreadfully. She cried, and Tom had to find his handkerchief and comfort her. Whilst he was patting the doll on the back, and wiping the sand out of her eyes, Amelia Jane was filling her pail from a pool.

She crept up behind Tom and tipped the pail of cold sea-water all down his neck!

'Ooooo-ow-oooo!' yelled Tom, jumping about twelve centimetres into the air with fright. 'You wicked doll, Amelia Jane! I told you not to do that!'

Amelia Jane thought it was such a funny joke that she rolled over and over on the sand, laughing.

The clockwork clown, who had seen all that had happened, remembered what she had said she would do to him, and he ran away to hide. He really was dreadfully afraid Amelia Jane would push him into a pool. Amelia looked for him. He had hidden himself under a clump of seaweed, so she couldn't see him – but she saw the brown teddy bear!

He was walking round the edge of a deep pool, looking at the crabs there. Amelia Jane crept up behind him. She gave him a push – SPLASH! The teddy landed in the pool and sat right down in the water.

'Ooooooo-ow-ooooo!' he gasped, his mouth full of salty water. Amelia Jane laughed till the tears ran down her face.

'You are very naughty and unkind,' said

the clockwork clown, poking his head out of the seaweed nearby. 'You are a most dreadful doll. Hi, Tom, come and help me push Amelia Jane into the water!'

'I shan't let you!' said Amelia Jane, at once. 'I shall paddle out to sea and sit on that rock over there. I am bigger than any of you, and I can get through the deep water easily. You won't be able to follow me. I shall be quite safe. Ha ha to you, clockwork clown!'

Amelia Jane had no shoes or socks on. She lifted up her red skirt and stepped into the waves. She waded out towards the big, big rock that showed itself some way out. It was covered with green seaweed. The teddy shook the water from his fur and ran after Amelia, splashing through the waves. But he was afraid of getting drowned, and he soon came back. Amelia was a very big doll, so she could easily get to the rock. The water did not come to more than her knees.

She reached the rock and climbed up. She waved to the others.

'I'm the king of the castle!' she shouted, dancing on the rock. 'You can't get me! I shall stay here and have a nice nap!'

She lay down on the soft green seaweed. The hot sun had dried it well. It was like a soft bed.

Amelia fell asleep. When the children came out to play, they didn't miss her. They had new spades and they wanted to dig a big castle.

They took no notice of any of the other toys, and didn't even see how wet the teddy bear was. They dug and dug and dug.

They had tea on the beach and then they dug again. When it was time to go home they collected their toys and set off up the beach. They had the clockwork clown, the bear, the toy soldier and the golden-haired doll – but they didn't have Amelia Jane. They had forgotten all about her.

And what about Amelia Jane? She was still asleep on the rock! The tide was now coming in – and it crept higher and higher over the rock. Soon it would reach Amelia's toes.

Soon a big wave would break right over the rock on top of Amelia – and then what would happen to her?

Amelia woke up. She sat up on the rock and looked round. When she saw how the tide was coming in, she was in a dreadful fright. The water was too deep to paddle through now. She couldn't swim. Oh dear!

Amelia Jane stood and yelled for help. 'Save me, somebody!' she cried. 'Save me!' But there was no one to save her. Poor Amelia Jane!

The other toys were sitting on a shelf, watching the children go to bed. Nobody thought of Amelia Jane. They were only too glad to forget her.

But when the children were safely in bed, Tom the toy soldier suddenly looked round –

and saw no Amelia. For a moment he wondered where she was – and then he remembered! She had been left on the rock – and the tide was coming in. Oooooo!

'I say, Toys,' said Tom, 'Amelia Jane's on the rock – and the sea will soon cover it right over!'

Now you might think that the clown, the golden-haired doll, and Tom would say, 'And serve Amelia right!' – but they didn't. They all looked at one another in alarm. Amelia was naughty – and she had played tricks on them – but they could not let anything horrid happen to her.

'What can we do?' asked the clown. He got down from the shelf and ran to the window. From there he could quite well see the rock on which Amelia stood, shouting for help.

'We must save her!' said the golden-haired doll.

'But how?' asked Tom.

'I know!' said the clown suddenly. 'We will take the children's toy ship – and sail it to the rock. We shall just get there in time. Hurry!'

The toy soldier and the clown caught hold of the toy ship, which lay on the floor. They ran out of the door with the golden-haired doll, and tore down to the beach. They put the boat into the water.

Tom got in. The golden-haired doll got in. The clockwork clown pushed off, and then jumped in himself. Tom arranged the white sails so that the wind filled them. The clown took the rudder and guided the little ship.

The tide was coming in fast. It was a long, long way now to the rock. Amelia Jane was very frightened. A big wave had washed right over the rock and had wetted her to the waist. Amelia was afraid that the next one would wash her right off the rock into the big sea.

'Help! Help!' she shouted, as another big wave came over the rock. Amelia held on to some seaweed. The sea wetted her right up to her shoulders. Oooh! It was so cold! She knew now how cold Tom must have felt when she poured water down his neck that morning!

'We're coming, Amelia Jane; we're coming!' shouted the toys. Amelia Jane heard them.

She looked over the waves and saw the three toys in the sailing-ship. It bobbed up and down as it came, for the sea was quite rough.

'Oh, you good creatures!' sobbed Amelia Jane. 'I don't deserve to be rescued – I was so unkind to you – but oh, I'm so glad to see you!'

The ship sailed quite near to the rock.

The clown was careful not to let it strike the rock – for that would mean a wreck. 'Jump, Amelia, jump into the ship!' he called. 'We can't come any nearer!'

Amelia Jane jumped. It was a good jump. She landed right in the middle of the boat.

It swayed about, and then as the clown turned it into the wind, the sails filled and the little ship sailed towards the shore again.

'You'll soon be safe home,' said the golden-haired doll kindly. 'Don't cry, Amelia Jane.'

'I won't tease you any more, any of you,' wept Amelia. 'It was so kind of you to remember I was on the rock and come to rescue me. Thank you ever and ever so much.'

The ship reached the sand. Tom jumped out and pulled it in. The golden-haired doll jumped out and helped poor, wet, cold Amelia Jane out. The clown jumped out last of all – and then they carried the ship back to the nursery again.

Tom took Amelia Jane down to the kitchen fire and dried her. Then back to the nursery they went, and soon fell asleep after their exciting day.

And was Amelia Jane kinder to the toys after that? Yes, very much kinder, all the time they were away at the sea. But alas! When they went back home again, Amelia Jane forgot all her good ways. Read on and you will see!

Amelia Jane and the Cowboy Doll

Now one day a funny little doll came to stay with the toys in the nursery. He was a cowboy doll. He didn't belong to the children who owned the nursery, he was just lent to them for a few days.

He was dressed in shaggy trousers, leather tunic, and a cowboy hat. He was very smart indeed, and the other toys were a bit afraid of him.

He could ride the old wooden horse, and made it gallop as fast as could be round and round the nursery! Once he even climbed up on to the big rocking-horse and made it rock

so fast that the horse *hrrumphed* in surprise,
and Nanny came running in to see what all
the noise was about!

The cowboy doll only just had time to hop
off the horse and lie down on the floor, where
he had been put by the children!

Another thing he could do was rather

marvellous. He had a long rope, and he could lasso anything with it that he liked! The toys would say to him, 'Lasso that tree on the toy farm, Cowboy doll!' And he would quickly throw his looped rope, and the end would neatly curl round the tree and topple it over!

He would lasso anything, even a pin stuck in the floor. And then, of course, Amelia Jane began to tell him naughty things to do!

'Cowboy doll, do lasso the clockwork mouse!' she whispered. 'Oh do! Look, he is over there, sniffing at that brick!'

The cowboy doll grinned. He had a most wicked face. He threw his rope neatly, and the loop at the end dropped right over the mouse's head – click!

The mouse gave a squeak of surprise and tried to run away, but the rope held him tight! He was very frightened.

'You shouldn't tell the cowboy doll to do that, Amelia Jane,' said Tom crossly. 'Why *must* you always get into mischief? Go and untie the mouse, quickly.'

'You go, Tom,' said Amelia Jane, giggling as she thought of more mischief. 'You are better at knots than I am!'

Well, the mouse was squealing so loudly that Tom really thought he had better go and help. So off he went, and Amelia Jane nudged the cowboy doll and whispered to him:

'Where's your other rope? Lasso Tom! He will get such a shock!'

So when Tom was bending over the mouse, trying to undo the loop of rope round him, there came a whizzing noise through the air, and another rope fell neatly right round

Tom's waist – click! It pinned his arms to his sides and he couldn't move! What a shock he got!

'You're my prisoner, Tom!' grinned the cowboy doll. 'Come over here!'

'I won't!' scowled Tom. 'Let me go!'

But he had to walk over to the cowboy doll and Amelia Jane because the cowboy pulled hard at the rope, and Tom had to come with it! He was so angry!

Amelia Jane thought lassoing was a lovely thing to do. She wanted to learn, and the cowboy doll said he would teach her.

'No, you are not to teach her,' said the golden-haired doll sharply. 'She is quite naughty enough without learning any more tricks. You are NOT to teach her!'

But the cowboy doll was not used to obeying other people, so he took no notice at all. He began to teach Amelia Jane, and she tried very hard to learn.

Soon she could throw a rope wonderfully well, and then, what a time the poor toys had! They never knew when a rope was going to come whizzing through the air after them, falling over their heads and shoulders! It was most worrying.

Amelia Jane practised hard, but she could not get quite so good at it as the cowboy doll.

Once she sent the rope flying through the air to catch the teddy bear as he walked along, and she missed him and got the rope round the chimney of the dolls' house.

Of course, she pulled too hard, and the chimney came off and fell on top of the bear's head. He was very cross indeed, and threw the chimney at Amelia Jane. She threw it back, and it almost hit the nursery cat on the nose. He was most surprised, and looked as if he would eat Amelia Jane. So she ran into the cupboard till the cat had gone down to the kitchen for his dinner.

The toys made her climb up to the dolls'
house roof and put the chimney on again.
She didn't like that at all, but she had to do it.
But even then she wouldn't stop lassoing
things.

She lassoed the humming-top when it was
spinning and made it fall down in a fright.
She threw her rope at a cow in the farmyard,
but caught the farmer himself and jerked him
so high in the air that he really thought he
was flying. He came down in the coal-scuttle
and was very angry about it. He told all his
cows to go and bite Amelia Jane, and she had
to climb up on to a shelf out of their way.

Another time she was very naughty indeed.
She thought she would lasso Mister Noah, who
lived in the wooden ark, and give him a shock.

He didn't like Amelia Jane, and wouldn't even say good morning to her when he met her. So Amelia waited for him to come out with all his animals.

'I'll lasso him now!' she whispered to the cowboy doll, with a grin. 'Watch me!'

She sent the rope through the air – whizz! But she missed Mister Noah, and the rope fell neatly round two tigers and two bears! How they roared and growled! They bit through the rope in a twinkling, left the line of animals, and tore over to where Amelia was standing with the cowboy doll.

The bears bit the cowboy doll's shaggy trousers so hard that they made a hole in them. The tigers scratched Amelia Jane on her legs, and you should have heard her yell!

'It serves you right,' said Tom, who had

been watching. 'We've told you ever so many times not to keep lassoing people.'

So for a little while Amelia Jane was good, but then something happened that made her bad again.

Somebody left a bag of sweets on the nursery mantelpiece. They belonged to one of the children, and Nanny had put them there.

Amelia Jane saw them and looked longingly at them, for she loved eating lots of sweets and chocolates.

How could she possibly get those sweets? She looked up at the mantelpiece and thought hard. The clock ticked away there. The goldfish globe winked back. It stood on the mantelpiece too, and was full of little black tadpoles that the children had found in the ponds. The china cat stood there too, watching the tadpoles wriggling about. And just by the cat was that bag of sweets.

'Oh, I know how I can get them!' said Amelia suddenly. 'I can lasso them with the cowboy's rope! Cowboy doll, where are you? Will you lend me your rope for a moment?'

The cowboy doll untied it. He always kept it tied round his waist. He gave it to Amelia

Jane and asked her what she wanted it for.

'I'm going to lasso that bag of sweets on the mantelpiece and get it down here!' said naughty Amelia. 'Then we'll share the sweets, Cowboy doll!'

'You'd better let *me* do the lassoing,' said the cowboy. 'You'll only go and lasso the cat or the clock, Amelia Jane!'

'No, *I* want to do it,' said Amelia. She looked up at the mantelpiece and swung the rope carefully. Whizz! It flew up to the mantelpiece! It missed the bag of sweets. It missed the clock. It just missed the china cat, but it caught the goldfish bowl! It fell neatly round it. The rope was tight – it pulled at the bowl – it toppled it over!

The watching toys gave a shriek! The water poured out of the bowl – all over

Amelia and the cowboy doll, who were just underneath! Tadpoles fell down their necks and flopped on to the floor! The bowl fell off too, and all the toys thought it would smash on the floor.

But no! It was too clever for that! It fell on to Amelia Jane's head, and there she stood, wet through, with the glass bowl on her head like an extra big hat!

Well, really, the toys simply couldn't *help* laughing! She looked too funny, and the cowboy doll, too, was soaked from head to foot. He was trying to get a tadpole which had fallen down his back and was tickling him dreadfully.

'Don't stand there laughing like this,' said Tom suddenly. 'Those tadpoles will die out of water. Quick, get something to put them into.'

The toys looked round for something but all they could think of was Amelia Jane's teacup. She was a big doll, so she had a very big cup. The toys put some water in it and then picked up the poor wriggling tadpoles. They found the one down the cowboy's neck, and took two from Amelia's neck as well. Dear, dear, what an excitement there was!

'What do you want to bother with silly tadpoles for, when Amelia Jane and I are all wet through!' cried the cowboy doll crossly. 'Please dry us.'

'It is more important to save the tadpoles than to bother about *you*,' said the clown. 'You can dry yourselves. It was your own fault that all this happened. Amelia Jane had no right to try and lasso sweets that didn't belong to her!'

Amelia squeezed out of her wet things and took the bowl off her head. It was rather a tight fit, and at first she thought she might have to wear the bowl all her life! That did give her a shock. She stood by the fire and tried to dry herself. She felt very cold and sad. The cowboy doll was wet too, and very angry.

'You *are* silly,' he said to Amelia Jane. 'Why didn't you let me do the lassoing? I could have got the bag of sweets then, but all we got was cold water and tadpoles!'

Amelia Jane said nothing, but dear me, when she found that her teacup was full of swimming tadpoles she was horrified.

'How can I ever drink out of my nice cup again?' she wept. 'It will be all tadpoley.'

'Amelia Jane, stop being silly,' said Tom sternly. 'You have made enough mischief without being stupid too. What do you suppose Nanny will say when she finds the tadpoles upset and the bowl on the rug?'

Nanny said a lot. She simply could *not* understand what had happened! At first she thought it was the cat who had done it. But no, Tibs had been in the kitchen all the time.

And then she caught sight of the cowboy doll who was standing in a corner, still very wet.

'I believe it's you, with your lasso, you naughty doll!' she said. 'Back you go to your own home!'

'Perhaps Amelia Jane will be good now that the cowboy doll has gone,' said the teddy to the clown. But I don't expect she will – do you?

Amelia Jane and the Plasticine

Now Amelia Jane had been good for a long time – so good that the golden-haired doll really wondered if Amelia was ill. But she wasn't ill; as the clown said, 'She was just boiling up for some more mischief!'

Amelia Jane had found the box of plasticine in the cupboard, and every night she played with the plasticine. She sat in a corner by herself, and the other toys took no notice of her at all. Amelia Jane was clever with the plasticine – she could make flowers and shells and tables and chairs and all kinds of things, just as you can.

And then, of course, naughty ideas began

to come into her mind. She had heard the teddy bear complaining that he had no tail. Suppose she made him one and stuck it on when he was asleep? He would think he had grown a tail, and what fun it would be to see him walking about proudly, showing off his beautiful new tail! What would he say when it came off?

Amelia Jane made a beautiful long tail of plasticine. It was brown to match the teddy bear's fur, and it had some pretty little blue spots here and there. Amelia Jane made some marks on it to make it look furry. It was finished at last. Amelia Jane grinned to herself and waited till she saw the teddy bear asleep in a corner.

Then she crept up to him with the plasticine tail. Nobody was about. Amelia Jane quickly

pressed one end of the tail on to the teddy
bear's back. It stuck nicely. Then the naughty
doll ran back to her place in the cupboard.

Presently the clockwork clown walked
along to talk to the bear. He saw the tail, and
he stared as if he couldn't believe his eyes!

'Hey, Teddy, Teddy, wake up!' he shouted in excitement. 'You've grown a fine tail! You have really!'

The teddy woke up with a jump. When he saw his new tail, curling round him like a cat's, he was so surprised that he couldn't say a word at first. Then he got up and bent himself over to have a look at it.

'A tail at last!' he said. 'A real tail! I always thought I might grow one, and now I have!'

'Tom, come and look at Teddy's beautiful new tail!' cried the clown. 'Do come! It's a fine one!'

Tom came, and the golden-haired doll – and Amelia went too.

'It's magnificent,' said Tom.

'It makes you look really handsome, Teddy,' said the golden-haired doll.

'How clever of you to grow it all by yourself!' said naughty Amelia Jane.

'Wasn't it clever of me!' said Teddy proudly, and he walked about showing his new tail to everyone. The clockwork mouse loved it, and the yellow duck said it was the longest she had ever seen. The bear was so happy that his boot-button eyes shone like lamps.

Not long afterwards the toys all sat down together to have cups of cocoa which the clockwork mouse had made for them on the stove in the dolls' house. Amelia Jane sat down beside the teddy – and whatever do you suppose she did? When the others were not looking she took hold of the bear's plasticine tail and with her clever fingers she made the end of it into a snake's head!

Fancy that! It looked exactly like a snake now, with its mouth open and two little holes for eyes!

Tom saw it first and gave a shriek! 'Oooh! Look! Your tail has turned into a snake, Teddy!'

The bear looked down in alarm – and when he saw the snake's head on the end of his tail he jumped up with a yell.

'Oh! Go away, snake, go away!' he shouted, and he ran to the other side of the room. But, of course, his tail followed him, for it was stuck on to him – and it looked as if the snake was running after him backwards! Poor Teddy! He was so frightened. He didn't like snakes at all, and to have his new tail turning into one seemed very dreadful to him.

Well, Amelia Jane laughed till she cried. It seemed funny to her to see the teddy bear rushing about with a snake-tail! The toys thought her very unkind to laugh, and the golden-haired doll shouted at her. But as Amelia Jane could shout twice as hard, that wasn't much good!

'Take your tail off, silly, if you're afraid of it!' called Amelia Jane.

'How can you take off a thing that's growing on you, stupid!' yelled back the teddy.

Amelia Jane ran to the bear and jerked at his tail. It came off quite easily, of course, for it was only plasticine. She threw it out of the window. The toys looked on in surprise. Then they all cheered Amelia.

'How brave of you, Amelia Jane! How good of you to do that! Did it hurt, Teddy?'

'Not a bit,' said Teddy, in surprise. 'Oh, thank you, Amelia Jane. The snake might have bitten you. You are very brave.'

Amelia Jane didn't tell the toys that the tail had only been plasticine made by herself. No – the naughty doll said nothing at all, but let the toys make a fuss of her.

I'll think of another plasticine trick, she thought gleefully. And, as you can guess, it wasn't very long before she did!

She made a set of nice little chairs, all with seats and backs and four neat little legs. Then she went to the paintbox and got the red paint. She painted those little chairs a bright red, and really, they looked simply lovely when she had finished. But, of course, you couldn't sit down on them because they were only made of plasticine and would crumple up at once!

But they didn't look as if they were made of plasticine when they were bright red. They looked like wooden chairs. Amelia Jane set them all out neatly in the middle of the floor.

'What are those chairs for?' asked Tom, in surprise.

'I'm going to have a party,' said Amelia Jane, and she got a table from the dolls' house. Then she called to the toys, 'Do come and join my party. The cakes haven't come yet but they'll be here soon. Just come and sit down and wait a while, Toys!'

The toys were pleased, for they loved any sort of a party. They came running over to Amelia Jane. Even the clockwork mouse came, and so did the old blue rabbit who had only one eye and no whiskers at all.

'Do sit down,' said Amelia, waving her hand to the red chairs. 'I hope there are enough seats for you all!'

Everyone sat down – but oh, what a shock they got! Tom's chair sank down at once, all its legs broken! He landed with such a bump on the ground! The golden-haired doll's chair tipped over backwards, and she bumped her head, and sat so hard on the plasticine that it stuck to her pretty blue frock. The clockwork mouse's chair crumpled up and he fell off and lost his key.

One by one all the red chairs gave way and tipped out the surprised toys. The clown didn't know what was happening and he clutched the back of his chair so hard that he squeezed up the plasticine it was made of and got it all over his arms! What a shock for him!

Amelia Jane thought it was so funny!
She laughed and laughed and laughed.

'It isn't funny,' said Tom angrily. 'Is this a trick instead of a party?'

'Yes,' said Amelia Jane. 'Oh, Tom you did look funny tumbling on to the floor!'

'I suppose there are no cakes coming after all,' said the clown fiercely. 'And I suppose too that it was you who stuck on the teddy bear's tail, and made it of plasticine! You are a wicked doll and you deserve to be frightened yourself!'

'Oh, you can't frighten me!' said Amelia Jane. 'I'm not afraid of anything!'

But she was, you know – she was afraid of beetles! The toys knew this, and they made up their minds to punish her! They went to the plasticine box, and the clown, who was clever with his fingers, made lots of big beetles, all with feelers on their heads and six legs under their bodies! The clown painted them black.

'This isn't a very kind thing to do,' said the clown, as he finished the last beetle, 'but really, Amelia Jane is so naughty that we must teach her a lesson. Where is she?'

'In the toy-cupboard, reading,' said the mouse. The clown took up the beetles and put them here and there on the floor. Then he called Amelia Jane.

'Amelia, Amelia, come quickly!'

Amelia Jane put down her book and rushed out of the cupboard – but when she saw those plasticine beetles she gave such a yell!

'Oooh! Ow! Beetles! Where have they come from? Take them away!'

The bear had tied a bit of black cotton to one beetle and he suddenly jerked this. The beetle jumped, and Amelia Jane screamed: 'It's coming after me! It's coming after me!

Oooooooh!'

She rushed back into the toy cupboard and crouched in the darkest corner. And do you know, she didn't come out of the cupboard for two days, so the toys had a lovely time playing together without wondering what mischief Amelia Jane was up to!

They have taken away the beetles, of course, but Amelia Jane doesn't know that! She'll think twice before she gets into mischief again, won't she!

Stop it, Amelia Jane

You might think that Amelia Jane would grow out of her bad ways, but she didn't. The day soon came when she felt bad again. It was the day that the pop-gun came to the nursery. The children had bought it and had been playing with it. It was great fun.

It was a wooden gun that had a cork fitted in at the end of it. When you pressed the trigger the cork flew out with a pop, but it didn't go far, because it was tied on to the gun with a piece of string. The children set up their wooden soldiers in a row and shot them down – bang! – with the pop-gun. The soldiers didn't mind, because it was what they were made for.

But when Amelia Jane got hold of the pop-gun that night and began shooting the cork at everyone, there was trouble!

'Stop it, Amelia Jane!' shouted the clockwork clown angrily, when his cap flew off into the coal-scuttle, shot there by the cork.

'Stop it, Amelia Jane!' cried Tom when he got the cork in his eye.

'Stop it, Amelia Jane!' squealed the engine. 'You're making my funnel loose with that cork – it keeps hitting it!'

But do you suppose Amelia Jane stopped? Of course not! She was enjoying herself far too much!

She shot at the castle of bricks and down they all fell! She shot at everything in the toy

farmyard, and trees, animals, and farmer
fell over flat. She shot at the clockwork mouse
and gave him such a fright that he ran into
the dolls' house and hid under a bed.
Nobody could get him out.

The clockwork clown called the other toys to him. 'We've got to stop Amelia Jane!' he said. 'I'm tired of all this popping. That cork doesn't do much damage but it stings all the same.'

'What about shooting Amelia Jane?' asked Tom eagerly. 'I'd like to do that.'

'Oh, she won't let that pop-gun go, you may be sure of that!' said the teddy bear.

'Well, there's a funny old gun in the cupboard that the children got out of a cracker,' said the clockwork clown. 'Why not shoot at her with that?'

'Because it doesn't shoot, silly,' said the bear. 'I've tried it heaps of times.'

'If it only made a pop it would do,' said the clown gloomily. 'We don't really want to shoot Amelia Jane – only to frighten her and make her stop popping the cork-gun at us.'

'Well, that old gun doesn't shoot and it doesn't make a pop either,' said Tom.

Then the bear had an idea. 'Listen!' he whispered, so that Amelia Jane wouldn't hear. 'I know where there is a packet of balloons! Couldn't we get them – and blow them up – and let Tom hide behind the curtain with them? Then I could hold the gun and point it at Amelia Jane – and at the same moment Tom could prick a balloon and burst it! Then it would go – *bang*! just like a gun – and frighten Amelia Jane!'

Everyone thought that was a splendid idea. So Tom got the packet of balloons and organised the toys to blow them up. They hid behind the curtains with the balloons. There were five. The bear found the gun and polished it up. Amelia Jane saw him and laughed.

'*That* old gun won't shoot!' she said, and she aimed the pop-gun at Teddy and shot the cork so hard that one of his ears went crooked. He was very angry.

'Oh, so you think this old gun won't shoot!' he said. 'Well, you're wrong!'

He pointed the gun at Amelia Jane – and at the same moment Tom dug a pin into one of the blown-up balloons behind the curtain.

Bang! went the balloon – and Amelia Jane gave a shriek. She really thought the gun that Teddy was holding had gone off!

'I'm shot! I'm shot!' yelled Amelia Jane in a fright. Everyone laughed. Teddy pointed the gun at the naughty doll again. Bang! went another balloon behind the curtains. Amelia Jane squealed and ran away.

'I'm shot again! I'm shot again!' she yelled. Teddy laughed so much that he nearly dropped the gun.

'Do you promise not to shoot anybody with that pop-gun again?' he said.

'No, I don't!' said Amelia Jane.

'All right then!' said Teddy, and he pointed the gun at her again. 'I'll go on shooting at *you* then.'

Bang! went a third balloon behind the curtain, and Amelia Jane screamed, 'I'm shot! I'm shot! He's shot me three times!'

Bang! went another balloon, and Bang! went the fifth balloon. Amelia Jane screamed so loudly that she quite deafened everyone. She fled into the toy-cupboard and wept bitterly.

'I won't shoot anyone any more. Here's the old pop-gun!' she cried and she threw it out of the cupboard to the teddy bear. 'Stop shooting me! I'm wounded everywhere!'

When Amelia Jane next came out of the toy-cupboard the toys stared in astonishment – for the big doll had bandaged her arms and legs and head. She did look funny!

'You shot me five times and wounded me,' said Amelia Jane in a hurt voice. 'You ought to be very sorry.'

But the toys laughed and laughed and laughed. How could she be wounded when it was only balloons that went off pop and not the gun? Oh, Amelia Jane, you are just a humbug!

Amelia Jane Up the Chimney

Into the nursery where naughty Amelia Jane
lived, came a little black kitten one day. Its
eyes were green, its tail was fat and long, and
its little paddy-paws were like velvet.

All the toys loved the kitten at once – but
Amelia Jane loved it
most of all! How
she cuddled it!
How she fussed
it! How she
stroked it from
ears to tail-tip and
tickled it under its
soft black chin!

The kitten belonged to the housekeeper. It was a pretty, gentle little thing, and it let the toys do what they liked with it. The teddy found it a buttery crumb to nibble. The clockwork clown turned head over heels seven times running to make it laugh. Tom found the dolls' hairbrush and brushed its fur till it shone.

But Amelia Jane wanted the kitten all to herself. She pushed away the other toys, and as she was bigger than they were they fell down, flop! That was the worst of Amelia – she was always so rough!

'*I* want this kitten!' said Amelia Jane. 'Tiddles, Tiddles, purr to me, and to no one else!'

'You are very selfish, Amelia Jane,' said Tom. Amelia Jane stuck out her elbow and pushed him again. Down he went, flip-flop! You couldn't do anything with Amelia Jane when she was feeling like that.

'This kitten is mine when it comes into our nursery,' said Amelia. 'Nobody else is to play with it then.'

Well, the kitten quite enjoyed being made a fuss of by Amelia, but it did want to play with the other toys sometimes. Amelia just wouldn't let it. She caught it and put it on her knee to stroke as soon as ever it ran over to Tom or Teddy.

And one day Amelia Jane thought she would like to dress the kitten up in clothes out of the dolls' chest-of-drawers! Quite a lot of clean dolls' clothes were kept there. It was really rather exciting to pull open the drawers and see the dear little coats and dresses, the fussy little bonnets with ribbons on, the socks and the shoes of all colours!

Amelia Jane pulled out the whole lot. She would, of course!

'Just look at that!' groaned Tom. 'Untidy creature! She'll never put those clothes back again neatly. We shall have to do that!'

Amelia Jane soon had all the clothes on the floor. She wondered which would fit the little black kitten. What fun to dress her up, she thought!

'This dress will fit you nicely, Tiddles,' she said, picking up a little red frock. 'Oh, you will look sweet in it. And this yellow coat will fit you, too – and this little bonnet with ribbons! Oh, what a darling kitten you will look!'

'Mee-ow,' said Tiddles, not at all liking the

idea of being dressed up by Amelia Jane. 'Mee-ow! I'm off!'

She shot to the nursery door – but Amelia Jane was too quick. She reached out her hand and caught poor Tiddles. 'You come here!' she said. 'I'm going to make you look really sweet!'

Well, Tiddles had to sit and be dressed up. First Amelia put on the little red frock and did all the buttons up the back. Then she put on the yellow coat. She tied a ribbon round Tiddles' waist. Then she put the bonnet on Tiddles' little black head and tied it on firmly.

'There!' she said. 'You are now a little dolly cat! You look lovely! Look, everybody!'

Everybody came to look. They couldn't help thinking that Tiddles really did look rather sweet – but Tiddles hated it! She struggled and wriggled and tried her hardest to scrape off her bonnet. She didn't like anything over her ears. She couldn't hear properly.

'Now, you shall look at yourself in the mirror, Tiddles,' said Amelia Jane, and she carried the dressed-up kitten to the big mirror.

The kitten looked at herself – and when she saw herself looking so very strange, with a bonnet on her ears, and a coat and dress hiding her black fur, she was afraid.

'Mee-ow! It isn't me!' she said in a fright, and she rushed away to go downstairs to the housekeeper. But Amelia Jane pushed the door shut.

'You're not to go away, Tiddles,' she said. 'We want to see you walking about nicely in your new clothes.'

But that was just what Tiddles couldn't and wouldn't do! She caught sight of herself in the mirror again and ran off in terror. She was so frightened that she meant to get out of the nursery somehow! But how could she? The door was shut. The window was shut.

'Oh, where can I go-ee-ow?' mewed poor Tiddles.

Now it was summer-time, so there was no fire in the nursery grate. Tiddles leapt over the guard, and in a moment she scrabbled up the chimney and was gone!

The toys stared at one another in alarm. What would happen to Tiddles up the chimney?

'Are you all right, Tiddles?' called Tom, sticking his head up the chimney.

'No-ee-oh-ee-ow!' wailed poor Tiddles, who was more frightened than ever up the dark chimney. She didn't dare to go up and she didn't dare to go down! Poor Tiddles!

The toys turned fiercely on naughty Amelia Jane. 'It's your fault!' shouted Teddy. 'You would dress her up and frighten her, just to amuse yourself. Now what are we to do?'

'Oh-ee-ow-ee-oh!' wailed Tiddles, up the chimney.

'I know! We'll make Amelia Jane go up the chimney and fetch Tiddles!' cried Tom. 'That's what we'll do!'

'I won't go,' said Amelia Jane.

'Oh yes, you will!' said Teddy. 'Come on, everyone. Push Amelia up the chimney!'

But they couldn't get the big doll to go. She just wouldn't be pushed. Just as the toys were going to have another push at Amelia, someone opened the nursery door. It was the housekeeper!

The toys at once lay down flat on the floor and kept quite still.

'I wonder where that kitten of mine is,' said the housekeeper, looking round the nursery. 'I thought I heard her mewing up here.'

'Oh-ee-ow-ee-ow!' wailed Tiddles from the chimney. The housekeeper looked astonished. 'I believe she's up the chimney!' she said. Then someone called her from downstairs and she hurried away.

Now Amelia Jane, although she really was a very naughty doll, was feeling most uncomfortable about poor Tiddles, for she

was fond of her.
As soon as the
housekeeper had
gone she ran across
to the fireplace,
climbed over the
guard, and looked
up the chimney.

'I'm going up the
chimney to rescue
Tiddles,' she said to
the surprised toys.
'I'm not going
because you tried to
push me up – I'm
going because I
don't like Tiddles
to be frightened.'

And up the chimney went Amelia Jane! The toys listened to her scrabbling her way up the long, dark, sooty chimney. Bits of soot fell down and one bit hit the teddy on the nose. 'The chimney wants sweeping,' he said.

'Looks as if Amelia is sweeping it!' said Tom, as another bit of soot rolled down.

At last Amelia Jane reached Tiddles who sat in a sooty corner, trembling. Amelia Jane put her arm round the kitten and hugged her. 'I'll help you to get down,' she said.

But dear me, that wasn't easy! Amelia Jane lost her way in the chimney, which joined all sorts of other chimneys here and there! Tiddles clung to her with all her claws and Amelia felt as if she was being pricked with twenty needles!

Now, very soon, the housekeeper came into

the nursery again, and who do you suppose was with her? The sweep! Yes – the housekeeper had told him a kitten was up the chimney, and he had said he would try to sweep her out very gently.

He screwed on the handles of his big brush one after another, and the brush went higher and higher up the chimney. Amelia Jane heard it coming. She didn't know the chimney was being swept. The toys had all rushed into the cupboard when they heard the housekeeper and the sweep coming upstairs! They hadn't had time to tell her anything.

'Oooh! What's this coming up the chimney?' suddenly said Amelia, as she dimly saw something black and hairy coming nearer and nearer. She didn't know it was the sweep's round black brush! 'Oooh! It's got whiskers! It's touched me! It's pushing me!'

Poor Amelia Jane! She was just as frightened as the kitten had been when it first ran up the chimney! She couldn't get away from the brush. It lifted her and the kitten up, up, and up!

'It's caught me, it's caught me!' wept Amelia. 'I didn't know a whiskery thing lived in chimneys!'

The brush swept Amelia Jane and the kitten right out of the chimney into the air! The kitten fell to the roof on its feet, and made its way carefully down to the kitchen, where the housekeeper took off the dolls' clothes in much astonishment.

Amelia didn't fall on her *feet*, because she wasn't a cat but a doll! She slid down the

roof. She hung for a moment in the gutter. She fell over the gutter – down, down, down – and into the prickly holly bush that grew just below!

'Ooh-ee-ow-ee-oh!' yelled Amelia, for the holly bush pricked her well! She scrambled out somehow and after a long time got back to the nursery.

But when she crept in at the door, what a fright she gave the toys! She was covered in soot from head to toe. Her clothes were all torn! Her face and arms were pricked and scratched!

'Oooooh!' yelled the toys and rushed to shut themselves in the cupboard. 'What is it? What is it?'

'It's me, Amelia Jane,' said Amelia, in a very small voice. 'I've come back.'

'Well, you look DREADFUL!' said Teddy, sticking his head out of the cupboard. 'For goodness' sake undress and have a bath and put on clean clothes!'

So Amelia did – but the clothes in the dolls' chest were much too small for her, and she did look funny walking about in things belonging to the baby doll!

'I shall be good in future,' said Amelia Jane. But I don't believe it, do you?

Amelia Jane and the Soap

Amelia Jane was feeling very bored. She had behaved herself for a whole week!

'But only because she hasn't been able to think of anything naughty to do,' said Tom to Teddy. 'As soon as she thinks of something she'll cheer up and be as bad as ever.'

Well, it wasn't long before Amelia Jane did cheer up. She had thought of something.

You see, it was like this – she had gone out for a nice walk, sitting in the dolls' pram, and she had been taken into the town. Now, racing up and down the pavement were two boys on roller-skates. What a pace they went!

Amelia Jane leaned out of the pram to

watch them. She thought it was a lovely game. She tried to see what the boys had on their feet, but they went so fast that Amelia Jane really didn't see what the skates were like.

How *do* they slip along so fast? she thought. I *would* like to skate like that. How I wish I could! I'd go round and round the nursery, and down the passage and back. My, wouldn't the toys stare!

Now, when Amelia Jane had an idea she just had to carry it out. So when she got back to the nursery she sat at the back of the toy-cupboard and thought hard.

'I want to skate,' she said to herself. 'I want to put something on my feet and slip along like those boys. I want to go fast! But what can I put on my feet?'

'What are you thinking so hard about?' asked the clockwork clown, poking his head in at the door.

'Never you mind,' said Amelia Jane.

'Tell me, and maybe I can help,' said the clown.

'Well, I'm trying to think of something nice and slippery,' said Amelia Jane.

'What about jelly?' said the clown.

'Don't be silly,' said Amelia.

'Well, soap,' said the clown. 'Nice wet soap! Why, the other day I got hold of some wet soap and squeezed it – and it shot out of my hand like lightning and hit Tom on the ear!'

Amelia Jane laughed. Then she stopped and thought quickly. Soap! Yes – that was really a *good* idea! If she got two nice pieces of soap, made them wet and slippery and tied them under her feet, she would be able to slip along just like those boys on skates! Good!

'I'll try it!' said Amelia Jane. So she ran out of the toy-cupboard and went to the nursery basin. She climbed up and looked to see if there was any soap there.

There was – and what luck! – it had broken into two nice pieces.

'Oooh!' said Amelia, in delight. 'Just what I want!'

She turned on the tap and wetted the soap till it was so slippery she could hardly hold it. Then she climbed down with it. The toys looked at her in amazement.

'What are you going to do?' said Teddy. 'Are you going to give yourself a good wash for once?'

'Don't be rude,' said Amelia. 'You'll see in a minute what I'm going to do.'

She took off a hair-ribbon and tore it in two. Naughty Amelia! Then she tied one piece of soap under her right foot and the other piece under her left foot. The toys stared at her as if they thought she was mad.

'Amelia, that's a funny way of washing your feet,' said Tom at last.

'I'm not washing my feet. I'm going to *skate*!' said Amelia proudly. 'Turn back the carpet, somebody. I must skate on the polished floor.'

The toys began to giggle. Really, what *would* Amelia Jane do next! Teddy and Tom turned back the carpet. Unfortunately they rolled the clockwork mouse up in it and had to unroll it again to get him out.

'Oh, do be quick!' said Amelia impatiently. 'I am simply longing to begin!'

At last the carpet was rolled right back. Amelia Jane began. She put first one foot out – slid along a little way on the soap – then put the other foot forward and slid too – and before the toys knew what she was about,

there she was, skating round the nursery on her soap-skates!

How the toys laughed! Really, it was too funny to see Amelia sliding along so fast on pieces of soap!

Amelia Jane tried to stop – but she toppled and fell over, bang! The toys roared. It was funny to watch Amelia sitting down, plop, glaring at them angrily.

'How dare you laugh at me!' cried Amelia Jane. 'I shall go and learn how to skate in the passage. There is a nice polished floor there – I shall slide beautifully!'

'No, stay here,' said the clown, in alarm. 'You know quite well that somebody may go along that passage and see you, Amelia Jane.'

'Pooh, everyone's in bed,' said Amelia, and this was true, for it was past midnight.

'Anyway, you won't be able to laugh at me there, if I fall down – for none of you dares to come into the passage.'

It was dark in the passage, for only a small light burnt there. Amelia slid out on her soap-skates and began to slide gaily up and down, up and down! The kitchen cat, hearing the noise, came creeping up the stairs, wondering if there was an extra-large-size mouse anywhere about.

He *was* astonished when he saw Amelia. He ran along the passage to see what she had on her feet. Amelia didn't hear him or see him, and she suddenly bumped right into him. Crash! She fell over and banged her head against the bedroom door.

'Sh! Amelia Jane! Sh!' whispered Tom, putting his head out of the nursery door.

But Amelia Jane
wouldn't hush. She
got up angrily and
shooed the cat away.
But the cat spat and
hissed, which scared
her a bit.

If Amelia Jane had been sensible she would
have run back to the nursery at once, but she
was so keen on skating that she once more
began to slide up and down, up and down, all
along the passage. She didn't hear Nanny's
bed creaking. She didn't hear Nanny creeping
to the door. She didn't even see Nanny
poking her head round the door – no, she
went slipping and sliding up and down on the
soap, having a perfectly lovely time!

Nanny couldn't make out who or what it

was, for the passage was so dark. But she could quite well see something going up and down the passage, skating quickly. She moved to the light switch to put a brighter light on.

Amelia Jane saw her then. Quick as lightning the doll slipped through the nursery door, fell over on the carpet, tore off the bits of soap, and ran to the toy-cupboard. She climbed in on top of the bear and the clown, who were very angry at being walked on.

But nobody dared to say a word! Suppose Nanny had seen what was happening? But when Nanny turned on the big light, all she saw was the kitchen cat sitting calmly by the wall.

'Good gracious,' she said, 'so it was *you* I saw, Puss, skating up and down the passage! What do you mean by doing that in the middle of the night, I should like to know! My goodness, what is the world coming to, when cats take to sliding up and down passages and waking everybody up! Shoo!'

She shooed the cat down the stairs, and he disappeared quickly, tail in air, boiling with rage to think that Amelia Jane had slipped off and left him to take the blame.

And in the morning, when Nanny saw the

messy bits of soap lying on the carpet, she was crosser than ever.

'Just look at that!' she said to Jane, the cleaner. 'It must be that cat. Slipped and slid down the passage all night long like a mad thing – and then went and tried to eat the soap out of the basin!'

Poor Puss got a scolding! Amelia Jane laughed at him – but she didn't laugh quite so much when the cat came downstairs and tore her new dress with his sharp claws.

'You'd better not skate any more with the soap, Amelia Jane,' said Tom. 'It's funny to watch you – but if you get other people into trouble it's not fair!'

So that was the end of Amelia Jane skating on the soap. I would have loved to see her, wouldn't you?

Amelia Jane and the Snow

It was snowing hard. The toys looked out of the nursery window and watched the big white snowflakes come floating down.

'The garden has a new white carpet,' said the teddy bear.

'Let's send the clockwork clown out to sweep the dust off it!' said Amelia Jane, the big naughty doll, with a giggle.

'Don't be silly, Amelia,' said the clown. 'You do say stupid things. There's no dust on a snow-carpet!'

'Isn't it pretty!' said the pink rabbit. 'I'd like to go and burrow in it!'

'Let's go and play in it!' said the golden-haired doll. 'It would be such fun.'

'Come on, then!' said Amelia Jane. She ran to the door, peeped out, and beckoned the others. 'Nobody's about. We'll slip out of the garden door and go to the bit of garden behind the hedge. Nobody will see us there.'

'Stop a bit, Amelia Jane,' said the clockwork clown. 'Put on a coat. It's very cold outside.'

'Pooh!' said Amelia impatiently. 'Don't be such a baby, Clockwork Clown! I shall be as warm as toast running about. I'm going!'

She ran off down the stairs. But the other toys stayed to put on hats, coats, and scarves. Even the clockwork mouse put a red handkerchief round his neck.

When they got out to the snow they found that Amelia Jane had already made herself a great many snowballs! She danced about as they came, and shouted in glee.

'Let's have a snow-fight! Come on! I've got my snowballs ready. Look out, clown! Look out, pink rabbit!'

The big doll threw a snowball hard. It hit the clown on the head and he fell over, plonk! Amelia Jane giggled. She threw a snowball at the golden-haired doll and hit her in her middle. The doll gave a squeal and sat down in the snow.

'Ooh, this is fun!' yelled Amelia. 'Come on, everyone, get some snowballs ready!'

But nobody could make such big hard snowballs as Amelia Jane. Amelia did enjoy herself. She pelted all the toys with snowballs, hitting them on the head and the chest and the legs – anywhere she could. She was quite a good shot, and the toys got very angry.

'Amelia Jane! Stop!' shouted
Tom. 'It isn't fair. Your
snowballs are three times as
big as ours, and you make
them so hard that they hurt.
Stop, I tell you!'

But Amelia Jane wouldn't stop. No, she
went on and on – and how she laughed when
all the toys turned and ran away from her
shower of snowballs!

'Let's leave her alone,' said the clown
crossly. 'She's too tiresome for anything.'

'But she'll follow us and go on snowballing
us,' said the mouse.

'No, she won't. She's found something else
to snowball,' said the teddy bear. 'Look!
She's snowballing the kitten!'

So she was. The kitten didn't mind the snowballs at all because she could always dodge them. She pounced on them as they fell, and Amelia Jane laughed to see her. She forgot about the toys.

'What shall we do?' said the golden-haired doll.

'Let's build a nice, round snow-house,' said the clown eagerly. 'It would be such fun to do that. I know how to. You just pile nice hard snow round in a ring and gradually make a round wall higher and higher. Then you make the wall slope inwards till the sides meet, and that's the roof!'

'Oh yes, that would be lovely!' said Tom. 'We could all live in the snow-house then.'

'But we won't let Amelia Jane come in at all,' said the clockwork mouse, getting a little snowball for the wall of the house.

'No, we won't,' said the golden-haired doll. 'It will punish her for throwing such hard snowballs at us.'

The toys worked hard at their snow-house. Soon the wall was quite high. It was a perfectly round wall. It grew higher and higher – and at last, as the toys shaped it to go inwards, the round sides met together and made a rounded roof.

The toys made a dear little doorway at the bottom. They were very excited, for the house was lovely. The clown ran to the pond, cut a square piece of ice, and ran back with it.

'What's that for?' asked the pink rabbit.

'A window, of course!' said the clown. He made a square hole in the side of the house and fitted in the piece of ice. It made a lovely window!

'Now let's go inside and be cosy,' said the golden-haired doll. So they all crowded into the dear little snow-house and sat down. It was lovely.

But just as the clockwork clown was telling a nice story, Amelia Jane came up. The kitten had gone indoors, and Amelia Jane wanted someone else to play with. She had looked and looked for the toys, but as they were in the snow-house she hadn't seen them.

She suddenly saw the house and came running up to it. She peeped inside the window.

'Oh, what a nice little house!' she cried. 'Let me come in, too!'

'No, Amelia Jane!' shouted all the toys. 'You are too big. Besides, we don't want you.'

'But I'm very, very cold,' said Amelia Jane, and certainly she was shivering.

'Well, you should have been sensible and put on your coat and hat as we did!' said the golden-haired doll.

'Oh, *do* let me come in!' begged Amelia, who hated to be left out of anything. 'Oh, do let me!'

'NO, NO, NO!' shouted the toys.

'Well, I'm *coming* in!' said Amelia crossly, and she began to push her way in at the door. A bit of the doorway fell down at once.

'Don't!' cried the clown, in alarm. 'You will break our house!'

'Serve you right!' said naughty Amelia. But the toys really couldn't bear to see their house broken.

'All right, all right, you can come in,' said

Tom. 'But wait till we get out, Amelia. You are so big that there isn't room for anyone else when *you're* inside!'

That pleased Amelia very much. She thought it would be lovely to have the house all to herself. She waited until all the toys had squeezed out of the house, and then she went in.

'Oh, it's lovely!' she cried. She pressed her nose to the window and looked out. 'It's lovely! It's a real little house. This shall be mine. You build another one for yourselves, Toys.'

But the toys were tired. They stared angrily at Amelia Jane.

'You are a very naughty, selfish doll,' shouted the teddy bear. 'First you snowball us till we have to run away. Then you take our house for your own.'

'I'm cold,' said the
clown, shivering. 'Let's
go and slide on the ice
for a bit. Perhaps
Amelia will get tired
of our house soon and
we can have it again.'

So they went off to
the pond and left
Amelia Jane by herself.

Amelia felt cold. She shivered and shook in
the little snow-house. 'I wish there was a fire
in this house,' she said to herself, 'then it
would be nice and warm. I'll make one! How
the toys will stare when they see I have a nice
fire to warm myself by! But I shan't let them
come in at all!'

She ran to the wood-shed and got some wood. She found some matches there that the gardener used when he lit a bonfire. She ran back to the snow-house. Soon the twigs were crackling loudly.

'What's that noise?' said the clown suddenly. All the toys stopped their sliding and listened. It came from their snow-house.

'Amelia Jane is lighting a fire there!' said Tom. Then the toys looked at one another – and began to giggle. They knew quite well what would happen if anyone lit a fire in a house made of snow! They ran up to watch.

'You can't come in, you can't come in!' shouted Amelia Jane. 'This is my house, and this is my own dear little warm fire! Oh, I'm so cosy! Oh, I'm so warm!'

The toys stood and watched. The fire

blazed up as the twigs burnt. There was a red glow inside the little house. It certainly looked very cosy. Amelia Jane put out her hands and warmed them inside the house.

But something was happening. The fire was melting the house! After all, it was only made of snow! The walls began to drip. The roof began to drip. The bit of ice that was the window disappeared altogether.

Amelia Jane felt the drips on her back and was cross.

'Who's pouring water on me?' she cried. 'Stop it, or I'll be very angry!'

Drip, drip, drip went the snow as it melted all around her. And suddenly the whole house fell in, for the snow was now so soft and melty that it couldn't hold together. The fire went out with a sizzle.

Amelia Jane disappeared, for the snow fell all over her!

'Oooh! Ow! What's happened?' yelled Amelia Jane, very frightened. She kicked about in the wet snow, and first her hands came out, and then her head. She sat in the snow and looked around.

'Ha ha! Ho ho ho!' roared the toys. 'It serves you right, Amelia Jane! You took our house – and you lit a fire and melted it – and it fell on top of you! Ha ha! Ho ho ho!'

Amelia Jane began to cry. She was wet through and very cold. She ran back to the nursery, leaving little wet marks all the way. She sat by the fire there and tried to get dry.

And very soon she began to sneeze: 'A-tishooo! A-tishoo!'

'Now I've got a cold!' she said miserably. 'Oh, why do I get naughty? Something nasty always happens to me when I do!'

'Well, just try and remember that, next time you feel naughty,' said Tom, giving Amelia his big red handkerchief.

But I don't expect she'll remember it, do you?

Amelia Jane Goes Mad

Once, when Amelia Jane, that big rascal of a doll, had been good for simply ages, she suddenly got tired of it and went quite mad! Never in her life had she been so naughty and, really, the toys got quite scared of her!

She was quite silly over water. She thought it was the greatest fun to fill the watering-can that belonged to the children, and lie in wait for any toy to come by at night.

She hid behind the curtain and waited till Tom came by. Then she tilted up the little green can and watered him! Goodness, how he jumped!

'It's raining!' he cried, and ran to get his

umbrella. But when he put it up, no rain fell at all, and everyone laughed at him.

'It never rains in the nursery, silly!' said the clockwork clown.

'Well, look at my wet hair,' said Tom, and he shook a shower of drops all over the clown. 'What do you call that if it isn't rain?'

The clockwork clown snorted, and went to visit the clockwork mouse over in the corner.

He didn't know that Amelia Jane was hiding behind the scuttle with the watering-can again! Just as he came by, whistling a merry little tune, Amelia tilted up the can – and, pitter-patter! down came the water over the startled clown.

He ran to get the umbrella then – and holding it carefully over him, he went back to the scuttle to find out what the water was. And there, of course, he found Amelia, laughing till the tears ran down her cheeks.

'Give me that watering-can, Amelia Jane,' said the clockwork clown sternly. When he spoke like that, he had to be obeyed, so Amelia meekly gave him the can. But she soon began to look around for some more water to play with.

This time she found a very naughty thing

to do. She found that if she stood on a chair by the wash-basin and turned on the tap, she could make the water spurt out all over the room by putting her hand under the tap. And she waited till the golden-haired doll came by, and then spurted the water all over her!

The golden-haired doll was angry, because the water went on her hair and took out the curl. So she was a straight-haired doll then, and everyone thought she looked most peculiar.

'I shall have to put my hair in curl-papers tonight, and they are so uncomfortable,' sighed the doll. 'Oh, how I wish I could *punish* Amelia Jane!'

Well, the clown climbed up to the basin, and with his strong hands he turned off the two taps so very tightly that not even Amelia Jane could turn them on again. So she couldn't play *that* trick any more.

Never mind! thought Amelia. I shall think of something else! What fun it is to play with water!

Well, she just couldn't get any water from the taps, and the toys felt safe. But Amelia Jane knew somewhere else to get water. Yes – the goldfish bowl was full of water for the two goldfish to swim in!

The goldfish lived on a table by the wall. Amelia Jane climbed up to the wash-basin and took the sponge from there. It was quite dry. Then she climbed up to the goldfish bowl and looked into the water.

'Can I borrow some of your water?' she asked the fish. And then, without waiting for

an answer, she dipped the sponge into the
water and made it dripping wet.

Amelia sat on the table and peeped over the
edge, waiting for someone to come by. The
rabbit and the dog were having a little walk
together and were coming near. Amelia Jane
giggled.

She waited until they were just underneath,
and then she squeezed the sponge gently.

Drip-drip-drip, drop-drop-drop! Large cold
drops of water fell on to the dog and the
rabbit. They were most surprised. They looked
up – but Amelia was no longer peeping over
the edge of the table, and they could see
nothing. They couldn't understand it.

'I'm wet,' said the rabbit, shaking himself.

'And I'm wet too,' said the dog, licking
himself. 'Where did it come from?'

'Can't imagine,' said the rabbit. 'Perhaps we are mistaken. Come, let us go on with our ramble.'

So on they went again, and Amelia Jane watched for them to come back near the table once more. Just as they passed, she held out her sponge and squeezed it hard again.

Drip-drip-drip, drop-drop-drop! Down came the water and soaked the dog and the rabbit. How angry they were!

'My ears are dripping,' said the rabbit.

'My whiskers are soaked,' said the dog. 'Let us tell the clown.'

Well, as soon as they complained to the clown, he knew quite well it must be Amelia Jane up to her water-tricks again, and he called to her very sternly:

'Amelia Jane! Will you stop soaking everyone? It isn't funny, it is very silly, for you will give everyone a dreadful cold. Where are you?'

But Amelia Jane wouldn't answer, though she was aching with trying to stop laughing. The clown was angry, and set out to look for her. He came too near the table and

Amelia Jane saw him.

'I can't help it!' she said to herself. 'I must throw this nice wet sponge at him!'

So she threw the sponge at the clown, and it hit him full in the middle. He fell down with a thud, and the sponge dripped wet on him from top to toe. He got up and stared angrily round. But he could not see Amelia Jane.

She was crouching down on the top of the table again, behind the goldfish bowl.

The clown went to talk to the doll, whose hair was now in curl-papers. The rabbit, the dog, Tom, and the clockwork mouse came too.

'It's time we stopped Amelia Jane,' said the clown. 'What about doing something to *her* with water? That would really be a good punishment!'

'But how can we?' asked the doll with curl-papers. 'If we throw the sponge at her, she'll only throw it back. And you've hidden the can so that she can't get it.'

Everybody thought hard. And then the clockwork mouse had an idea! He was only a small toy, but he sometimes had surprisingly big ideas.

'I know!' he said. 'What about a siphon of soda-water?'

All the toys stared at him as if he were quite mad. '*You* know!' said the mouse. 'The thing that the big people keep in the dining-room, and squirt into a glass when they want a drink. I've seen them. What about getting one of those out of the kitchen where they are stored, and having a squirt at Amelia Jane? If she's so fond of water, she might like a bit of squirting!'

The toys laughed. The clockwork clown and the rabbit went out of the nursery and down the passage to the kitchen to see if they could find a siphon. They found one quite easily in the larder. It was terribly heavy. They had to fetch the dog to help them to carry it back to the nursery.

Amelia Jane had got down from the table and was busy tying a new hair-ribbon in her yellow hair. She was surprised to hear the heavy bumping as the toys carried the siphon in at the door. She turned round and laughed.

'Whatever have you brought that great ugly thing for?' she asked.

'Do you want to know?' said the clown, bringing it right up to her. Before she could answer, the toys pressed on the handle of the siphon, and the soda-water squirted out with a tremendous hissing noise, right into Amelia Jane's surprised face!

Good gracious! She was so startled that she fell over!

The toys squealed with delight and squirted her on the ground. She got up and ran away in a dreadful fright. But the toys followed her,

and squirted her all the way! Oh dear, oh dear! Poor Amelia, what a shock she got! The siphon made such a noise, and the water soaked her and ran down her neck and quite took her breath away!

'Do you like water so much now?' cried the clown. 'Do you think it is nice to be soaked? Squirt-squirt-squirt! How do you like to be watered, Amelia Jane?'

Well, Amelia certainly did not like it! She squealed and screamed and made such a noise that the toys were really afraid she would wake up everyone who was asleep. So they stopped squirting her and quietly took the siphon back to the kitchen.

Poor Amelia Jane! She had to take off all her clothes, even her underwear, and dry them by the fire. Even her body was wet, and she had to dry that too, turning herself round and round all night long! I don't think she will play with water again, somehow!

And nobody in the house could think where all the soda-water out of that siphon had gone to. Amelia Jane isn't likely to tell them, anyhow!

Amelia Jane and the Matches

This is the tale of Amelia Jane and the matches.

Now all boys and girls are warned by their fathers and mothers never to play with matches. And with toys it is just the same. They must never play with matches, in case they get on fire and burn themselves.

But you can guess that Amelia Jane didn't care about any danger! No! If she could get hold of matches you may be sure she would!

There were never any matches left in the nursery, till one day when Jane lit the fire and forgot to put the matches back in her apron pocket, as she usually did.

Jane left the box of matches on the mantelpiece and Amelia Jane saw it first, of course because she was quite the tallest toy in the nursery.

'Oooh!' she said, pointing upwards. 'Matches! If only I could get them!'

'Don't be naughty,' said the clockwork clown at once. 'You know that children and toys must never touch matches.'

'Pooh!' said Amelia Jane rudely.

'Don't pooh at me like that!' said the clockwork clown. 'It's rude.'

'Pooh, pooh, pooh!' said Amelia Jane. So you can guess she was in one of her naughty moods again.

She stood and thought for a minute. Then she remembered how the cowboy doll had taught her to throw a lasso round anything and jerk it near. If only she could make a loop of rope and throw it carefully, she could get those matches down easily.

She ran to the string-box and opened it. The teddy bear saw her. 'If you're thinking of lassoing those matches and getting them down, just let me remind you what happened last time you tried your hand at that!' he said. 'You lassoed the bowl of tadpoles, and got them all down your neck.'

Amelia Jane took no notice. She got out a long piece of string and made a loop-knot at the end. Then she stood beneath the mantelpiece and threw the string neatly upwards, holding one end in her hand.

'Ooooh!' said all the toys in surprise, because, will you believe it, Amelia Jane got the loop right round the box, and it fell almost at her feet when she pulled the string!

'Aren't I clever!' said Amelia proudly.

'No, you're not, you're just lucky,' said the clockwork clown. 'You're not to touch those matches, Amelia Jane.'

'Pooh!' said Amelia, and she opened the box. 'Now, who wants to see me strike a match?'

The toys felt frightened. They knew quite

well that matches can set fire to things and burn them. They ran to the toy-cupboard and crept inside, all except the clockwork mouse, and he did badly want to see a match struck.

'I'd like to see some matches struck, please, Amelia,' he said, and he ran nearer.

'Well, you shall see a whole lot struck!' said the big doll. 'The others have all run away, the sillies. You and I will enjoy ourselves!'

Amelia opened the box. She took out a match. She struck it hard on the side of the box. Fizzz-zzz-zzz! The match lit and Amelia Jane held it up in the air, watching the bright flame.

The clockwork mouse liked it very much indeed. He thought it was most exciting.

'Please, please, let me light one too,' he begged.

'Amelia Jane, if you let the mouse strike a match we'll all come out of the cupboard and punish you,' shouted the clockwork clown. 'He's too little to do dangerous things like that.'

'All right, all right!' said Amelia, striking

another match. 'I shan't let him. Besides, I want to strike them all myself!'

But before Amelia Jane could strike any more matches there came the sound of steps on the landing outside. The toys flopped down. Amelia ran to the cupboard, throwing the box of matches into a corner. The clockwork mouse ran into the brick-box. So when Jane looked into the nursery, there was no one to be seen at all. Everything was quiet. She had come to put some fresh flowers on the table. Then she dusted round a bit and went downstairs again.

The toys didn't come out for a long time – not until it was night, for they were afraid of being caught. The first toy that came alive was the clockwork mouse. He saw the box of matches in the corner and was pleased.

He ran to them and pushed them along with
his nose till he came to a slipper. He popped
them into the slipper.

Aha! he thought. Now no one will know
where they are, and I can strike as many as
I like when the others are not looking!

Now when all the toys came out of the

cupboard they looked very stern indeed. They were angry with Amelia Jane. She had no right to teach the clockwork mouse to play with matches!

The toys sat round Amelia in a circle, and scolded her.

'We shall none of us talk to you for a week,' said the teddy bear.

'We shall not play with you at all,' said the clockwork clown.

'You will not have any of the sweets out of the toy sweet-shop,' said the golden-haired doll.

'And we have hidden your fine new bonnet so that you can't wear it when you go out,' said the pink rabbit.

'Pooh!' said Amelia Jane – but not in a very poohy voice. She was upset. She hated not

being talked to or played with. It would be
horrid not to have any sweets. And oh, fancy
hiding her lovely new bonnet so that she

couldn't wear it! Amelia Jane felt like crying.
She walked over to the window-seat and sat
there, sniffing hard. She was very unhappy.

Suddenly the toys heard a curious noise.
Fizz–zz–zz–zz!

It was the clockwork mouse striking a match all by himself. The toys stared at him in horror. He struck another and squeaked in delight.

But oh, my goodness me, what do you think happened?' His whiskers caught alight! Yes, they really did, and the poor little mouse found himself on fire, with flames burning each side of his little face!

'Sizzle-sizzle!' went his fine whiskers. The mouse squealed in fright and flung away the lighted match. Oh dear – it fell on to an open book and the pages caught alight! The book flamed up, and set light to the brick-box nearby.

'Crackle-crackle!' went the flames merrily. 'Crackle-crackle! We're going to eat the book! We're going to eat the brick-box! Then we'll eat the carpet – and the chairs – and the toy-cupboard – and all the toys – and the whole house! Crackle, crackle, crackle!'

It was dreadful. The toys stared in horror

and couldn't move even a paw, they were so frightened. No wonder they had been warned against playing with matches. This was what happened when they disobeyed!

'Eee-eee-eee!' squealed the poor little clockwork mouse, his whiskers burning all away. He ran to and fro in pain and fright. All the toys watched and trembled dreadfully.

And what about that big, naughty doll, Amelia Jane? Yes – she was watching too, her face pale with fright. Poor, poor little mouse – how she wished she hadn't shown him how to strike matches! And oh, that book – and the lovely brick-box! Whatever would happen to them all?

'Well, I began it, so I must try and stop it!' cried Amelia Jane. 'I remember hearing someone say that if anyone got on fire they should be rolled round tightly in a rug to put the flames out. Where, oh, where is a rug?'

'In the dolls' pram!' yelled the teddy bear, who was still too frightened to move.

Amelia Jane ran to the dolls' pram. She snatched up the thick blue rug there and rushed to the little clockwork mouse. She threw the rug all round his little grey body and rolled him up tightly in it, head, tail, and all! She felt the flames trying to burn her hands, and they hurt her, but she didn't stop. She meant to save the little mouse!

The thick rug squashed all the flames out. They died away. There were none left. The clockwork mouse wasn't on fire any more.

But the book and the brick-box were still burning away. Amelia Jane left the mouse and ran to the basin with a jug. She stood on

a chair, turned on the tap and filled the jug. Down she climbed and rushed to the brick-box. She threw the water over the flames.

'Sizzle-sizzle!' they said, and died out. They could not go on burning when water was thrown over them. Then Amelia fetched another jug of water and threw it over the burning book.

'Sizzle-sizzle!' said the flames again, and went out. The fire was gone!

The toys came round, looking quite pale. Amelia Jane sat down and began to cry.

'I wish I hadn't touched the matches, I wish I hadn't!' she sobbed.

'I've got no whiskers now!' wept the poor little clockwork mouse. Sure enough, he hadn't – and he did look funny without them. What a noise Amelia Jane and the mouse made, sobbing together!

'You'll never speak to me or play with me again,' wept Amelia, looking round at the toys. 'I might as well go away from here and never come back.'

'Now listen, Amelia Jane,' said the teddy bear, putting his arm round her. 'You did a very wrong thing, and it has caused a lot of damage – but you have done your best to put it right, and you were brave when all of us were too afraid to do anything.'

'So we will have to forgive you,' said the clown. 'We were angry with you when you were bad, but we think you are brave too, so cheer up.'

'What about the mouse's whiskers, though – and the burnt book – and brick-box?' wept Amelia.

'The mouse will have to do without his whiskers,' said Tom. 'The book was very old and torn, so perhaps it won't matter being burnt; and as for the brick-box, it's only the lid that has been burnt, and I can make a new one with the carpenter's set in the toy cupboard. But look at your own hands – and the front of your dress! They are burnt too!'

'It serves me right,' said Amelia Jane. 'I'll put some good ointment on my hands, and I'll have to go about with a burnt bit of dress in front. Oh, I'm so glad you've forgiven me, Toys! I won't be naughty again.'

Well, the toys didn't believe that, of course – they knew Amelia Jane too well! But they were soon good friends again, and, secretly, they couldn't help admiring Amelia Jane for putting out the fire so quickly, and saving the little mouse.

'She's like the little girl in the nursery rhyme,' said the bear to the clown. '*You* know – when she's good she's *very, very* good – but when she's bad she's horrid!'

Amelia Jane
Is Naughty Again

Contents

Amelia Jane's Necklace

You remember Amelia Jane, don't you, the naughty doll who lives in the nursery with Tom the toy soldier and the teddy bear and all the other toys?

She's still there – and still naughty, though she does sometimes turn over a new leaf. But, as Tom says, it's never a very *big* leaf, and doesn't seem to last long.

Now, one day Tom went exploring in the toy-cupboard, and he found an old cardboard box. It rattled when he shook it, and he wondered what could be inside.

'Open it and see,' said the teddy bear. So Tom opened it. He and the bear stared at

what was inside. They didn't at all know
what the little brown things there were.

'Are they nice big beads?' said Tom.

'They might be something to eat,' said the
bear, but he couldn't even nibble a hole in
one of the smooth brown things.

The sailor doll strolled up to look. 'Oh, they
are *acorns*,' he said. 'Didn't you know *that*?'

'What are acorns?' asked Tom, who had never heard of them in his life.

The sailor doll didn't know, but he pretended to. 'Oh, they are things that can be used for a bead necklace,' he said, remembering that he had once seen the children stringing them together. 'Yes, acorn beads, I suppose. They would make quite a nice necklace, wouldn't they?'

'Oh,' said the bear suddenly. 'Tom, do you think *I* might have an acorn necklace to wear round my neck? Ever since I lost my blue bow I've felt very cold about my neck. I should so like a necklace. It would keep my neck very warm.'

'Well, Teddy, we'll thread you one,' said Tom, who was always very kind. 'Now let me see – what do we want for threading beads?'

'A sharp needle – and some string,' said the sailor doll. 'Look – somebody has already made holes through the acorns, ready for threading. They must have done that and then forgotten all about them.'

Amelia Jane came up, full of curiosity. 'What's that you've got?' she said.

'Acorns,' said Tom, and turned away. He wasn't pleased with Amelia Jane. She had knocked his hat off that morning and pulled out a tuft of his hair to make whiskers for another toy.

'Acorns! What are they?' said Amelia.

'BEADS!' said the sailor doll. 'But NOT for you. For the teddy bear, because he's lost his blue bow.'

'Well, I've lost the lace out of my shoes,' said Amelia Jane. 'I don't see why I shouldn't have the beads as much as the bear.'

'What's losing a shoe-lace got to do with having a necklace?' asked Tom.

'Quite a lot,' said Amelia, who could always argue for hours. 'You see, if I can't have a shoe-lace, I might as well have a neck-lace.'

'Don't be silly,' said the bear. 'You always want everything. Well, you're not going to have *this*!'

The sailor doll, the bear and the toy soldier took the box of acorn beads away to a corner. Amelia Jane followed them. They wondered where to get a needle and thread.

'There are some in the work-basket,' said Amelia Jane. Tom climbed up to the table to get a needle and some strong thread. He found a little roll of string there and decided that would do nicely.

Down he came. But, of course, nobody could thread the little needle with the thick string.

'Oooh!' said Tom. 'That's the second time I've pricked myself.'

'Bother this,' said the bear, trying hard to push the end of the string through the needle eye. 'It won't go. Oh dear – now *I've* pricked myself!'

'Let *me* try,' said Amelia Jane, and she took up the string. She saw at once that it wouldn't go through the eye of the little needle. She looked at the holes in the acorns. They were big – quite big enough to take the string without a needle to drag it through.

'*I'll* show you!' said Amelia, and she picked up an acorn in her left hand. She ran the

string through the hole in it and then picked
up another.

'See? Quite easy! You are always so stupid.
I'll thread the whole lot now.'

She threaded all the acorns very quickly. She really was clever at things like that.

'Thanks,' said Tom, when she had threaded the whole lot.

'That's fine. Now I'll put the necklace round the bear's neck. It will suit him.'

But Amelia Jane put it round her own! And what is more, she tied the string very tightly into a firm knot.

She grinned round at the toys. 'It's mine!' she said, touching the necklace. 'I threaded it, didn't I?'

Well, what was to be done about *that*? Tom was so cross that he held Amelia Jane's arms, whilst the sailor doll tried to undo the knot of the necklace. But he couldn't possibly, because it was much too tight. So they had to give it up and marched off to the toy-cupboard very crossly indeed.

'Mean thing! She's always doing things like that,' said the bear. 'And I did so want a necklace for my throat, now I've lost my blue bow. I do feel upset.'

'It's just like Amelia Jane,' said the sailor doll, gloomily. 'Why didn't we think of her putting it on as soon as she'd finished it? Now we shall never have it, and she'll keep on and on saying, "Look at my beautiful new necklace!"'

That is just what Amelia Jane did say,

of course! Whenever anyone came to visit the toys, she would show them her necklace. 'Isn't it lovely?' she would say. 'It's made of acorns. I've heard that they are very, very precious. I made this necklace all by myself!'

Now, that summer was very, very hot. The nursery children went away to the sea, and the toys were left by themselves in the nursery.

'I can't stand this heat,' said Amelia Jane, one day. 'I'm going out into the garden – and I'm going to undress and get into the pond to cool myself. It's no use saying I mustn't, because I'm GOING to!'

Well, she did, of course. She took off all her clothes except her underwear, which was sewn on and wouldn't come off, and she got into the water at the edge of the garden pond.

She lay right down in it, with her head against the edge of the pond, and kicked and splashed in joy.

'It's lovely! It's so cold!' she called. 'Come along and enjoy yourselves, toys! Ooooh! This is delicious!'

The other toys paddled. They were afraid of undressing and getting right into the water in case somebody came in quickly and didn't give them time to dress and get back to the toy-cupboard. But Amelia Jane never cared about things like that.

She spent all day in the water, and the next day, too, lying there in her underwear and acorn necklace, enjoying herself thoroughly. She frightened the sparrows who came to bathe, and she splashed the freckled thrush when he flew down. She really was full of mischief those hot, summer days, and soon no toy liked to go near the pond for fear of being soaked to the skin by Amelia Jane.

Now, if acorns are soaked in water for hours and hours they begin to grow! An acorn is the seed of an oak tree, and if it is made damp, it wants to put out a root and a shoot, like all seeds.

And Amelia Jane's acorns were no different from any other acorns. When they felt the water round them, soaking into them, they rejoiced, and grew fat. They wanted to burst their skins, and put out little white roots and shoots, to grow into tiny oak-trees!

Nobody noticed that the acorns had grown fat. Amelia Jane didn't, of course, because nobody can see what is tightly threaded round their neck. But when the acorns burst

their skins a little, and put out white roots,
Tom saw them, and gave a scream.

'What's the matter?' said the bear.

Tom pointed to Amelia Jane's neck. 'Look!
Her necklace is growing white worms! Ugh,
how horrible. Worms down her neck!'

Everyone stared at Amelia Jane's neck.

She didn't like it at all. 'What's the matter?' she said. 'What's all this about worms?'

'Oh, Amelia Jane – it's quite true. Your necklace has got white worms in it,' said the sailor doll. 'They are wriggling out of the acorns. That's where they live, I suppose! Oooh, how horrible!'

'I don't believe you,' said Amelia, and she put up her hand to her necklace. She touched one or two of the growing white roots and gave a scream. 'Oh, I touched a worm! I did, I did! Oh, whatever shall I do?'

'Well, you *would* take the necklace,' said the bear, quite pleased. 'It's your own fault. You shouldn't have been so selfish.'

Amelia Jane stood trembling in the nursery. 'Will they crawl down my neck?' she said, looking pale.

'I expect so,' said the bear, who was quite enjoying himself. 'If I were a worm I'd crawl all over you.'

Amelia screamed again. 'Don't! I can't bear it. Take them away! Undo my necklace, quick!'

'Certainly not,' said the sailor doll.

'You wanted to wear it, and you jolly well can!'

'I'll undo it myself,' said Amelia, but she couldn't. That knot was tied so tightly that she couldn't possibly undo it herself. And nobody else would.

'You can go on wearing worms,' said the bear. 'Fancy wearing a worm necklace! Ha, ha! It suits you, Amelia.'

'Please, please do untie the knot,' begged the big doll. 'Where are the scissors? We can cut the string.'

But there were no scissors to be found. The work-basket had gone, and not one of the toys had any scissors of their own. So Amelia

had to go on wearing her peculiar necklace.

She was very, very miserable. The toys watched the 'worms' growing longer each day, as the roots pushed out from the acorns. 'They're getting bigger, Amelia,' said the bear. 'And longer. And fatter. Oooooh! I wonder if those worms will get hungry, Amelia Jane, and nibble you.'

Amelia sobbed with fright. What could she do? The toy soldier was sorry for her and tried to undo the knot, but he couldn't. 'Go out into the garden and see if the worms will drop down and join the brown worms in the grass,' he said.

So Amelia went out and stood in the garden. And whilst she was there the string, which had got rather wet and rotten at the front of her neck, suddenly broke. And down fell all the acorns, with their funny white roots and tiny shoots.

'They've gone!' yelled Amelia, and fled

indoors. The toys went out to see. There lay the acorns, with the white 'worms' sticking out of them.

'Let's bury them in the ground, then perhaps these white worms will go and join their brother brown worms,' said the sailor doll.

So they dug little holes and put the split acorns, with their roots and shoots, carefully in the earth.

And, would you believe it, they all grew into tiny little oak-trees, with strong, white roots delving deep into the ground, and little shoots that bore leaves in the sunshine!

But Amelia Jane didn't know that. She never went near that part of the garden, in case those white worms saw her and went after her.

Poor Amelia! She says she is never going to wear a necklace again, and I don't expect she ever will. The bear says it serves her right – but it really was very funny, wasn't it?

Amelia Jane and the Ink

Amelia Jane was in a very bad mood, and when Tom the toy soldier asked her to play with him, she pushed him away and started to quarrel with him.

'You can't play games,' Amelia Jane shouted. 'You are so stupid.'

'I'm not stupid,' said Tom.

'Yes, you are,' said Amelia Jane.

'Stop it, you two,' said the bear. 'Don't take any notice of Amelia Jane, Tom.'

'It's difficult not to,' said Tom.

The toys began to talk together, but they wouldn't talk to Amelia. When she was in one of her silly moods, they just took no notice of her.

She didn't like that. 'Be quiet, stop talking,' she said. 'I'm going to write a letter.'

'Well, write it. We don't care!' said the bear. 'Who are you going to write it to?'

'Father Christmas,' said Amelia.

'Well, tell him to come and take you away and put you in his sack, and pop you into a stocking in some other nursery,' said Tom.

Amelia Jane was angry. 'You're unkind,' she said. 'I shall write to him – but I shall ask him to come and take *you* away. So there. You'll be sorry you were nasty to me, then.'

Tom felt rather frightened. He wasn't at all sure that Father Christmas might not do what Amelia said.

'Father Christmas never reads any letters unless they are written in ink,' he said at last. He knew Amelia Jane only had a pencil to write with.

She looked at him. He said it so loudly that she thought it must be true. 'All right!' she said. 'I'll write my letter in ink then!'

The toys stared at her in horror. Not even the children in the nursery were allowed to write in ink. Their mother said they were not old enough. So the ink was always kept out of reach on the mantelpiece.

'Amelia Jane! You'd never dare to write in *ink*!' said the bear.

'Wouldn't I?' said Amelia. 'Well, you just see! I shall write my letter in ink, with a pen, and I shall blot it properly and everything.'

'You can't reach the ink,' said the bear.

'I can,' said Amelia.

'You're not to,' said the clockwork clown.

'I just shall then,' said Amelia. She went to the coal-scuttle and climbed up on top of it. From there she climbed on to the top of the nursery fireguard, which went all round the hearth.

Then she leaned on the mantelpiece to try and reach the bottle of ink. She just could!

She edged it carefully towards her. Then she took the bottle into her hands.

'I've got it!' she cried. 'Look!'

She turned to show the toys – and lost her balance! She fell off the guard on to the hearth-rug – bump! The bottle of ink flew into the air and then fell bang on to Amelia's head. Its cork shot out and the ink poured all over Amelia's face! Some went into her mouth. She spat it out at once.

'Poof! It's horrid!'

The toys stared at Amelia Jane in horror. Her face was blue all over. She did look funny. The toys didn't like her at all. She didn't look like Amelia Jane. She looked rather fierce and wild.

'What's the matter?' said Amelia Jane, as the toys began to edge away from her.

'We don't like you. You're all blue in the face now,' said the bear.

'As blue as the sailor doll's trousers,' said Tom.

'You frighten me!' squealed the clockwork mouse, and raced into the toy-cupboard as if a cat were after him.

'Don't be silly,' said Amelia, trying to wipe her face with her hand. It made her hand blue. She stared at it and wondered what she looked like. There was a mirror over the bookcase. Amelia Jane pushed a chair by the bookcase, climbed up it and stood on the top of the bookcase. She looked at herself in the mirror there.

'Oh! Oh!' she squealed. 'It isn't me! It isn't me! I'm somebody else! Oh, where have I gone? It isn't me!'

The toys looked at her. Certainly Amelia Jane didn't look like herself at all.

'There's only one thing to do, Amelia,' said Tom. 'You'll have to scrub your face!'

'Yes, I will, I will,' sobbed poor Amelia, taking another look at herself in the mirror, and then scrambling quickly down to the floor. 'Tom, get a scrubbing-brush, quick.'

Tom went to the basin and climbed up on to the chair below. He knew there was a

nail-brush there. He took it and rubbed it on the soap. Then he climbed down and went to Amelia Jane.

'Shall I do the scrubbing?' he asked. Amelia nodded. So Tom began to scrub her face. How he scrubbed!

'The soap's gone in my eye!' yelled Amelia Jane. Tom took no notice.

'Now it's in the other eye!' sobbed Amelia. 'Don't scrub so hard.'

Tom went on scrubbing. 'You're scrubbing my face away,' wailed poor Amelia. 'Don't scrub my nose so hard. Oh, it'll come off, I know it will!'

All the toys stood round, grinning. They couldn't help thinking that it was a very good punishment for Amelia Jane, after quarrelling with Tom so much, and trying to take the ink.

How he scrubbed! Amelia sobbed and cried, and her eyes smarted with the soap, but Tom wouldn't stop until her face was perfectly clean again. All the toys cheered him on. At last his arm ached and he put down the nail-brush.

'There,' he said, 'now you're all right.'

'Thank you,' sobbed Amelia. 'Oh dear, oh dear, why ever did I say I'd write in ink? Look at the mess on the hearthrug!'

Poor Amelia had to set to work and scrub that clean too. She put the empty bottle of ink back on the mantelpiece, feeling very guilty.

'You ought to look in your money-box and put some money by the bottle to pay for some more ink,' said the bear.

So Amelia looked in her money-box and

put five coins on the mantelpiece by the bottle. The children found them there the next day, and they *were* surprised!

'Where did this money come from?' they wondered, and they turned to look at the toys. 'Goodness – isn't Amelia's face clean! Whatever has happened to it?'

They might have guessed when they found that their nail-brush was blue with ink – but they didn't!

As for Amelia Jane, she told Tom she was sorry she had quarrelled with him – so one good thing came out of her naughty prank, after all!

Amelia Jane's Boomerang

Amelia Jane found a toy boomerang at the back of the cupboard. Do you know what a boomerang is? It is a bit of curved wood made in such a way that it will always come back to the one who throws it.

You can see the boomerang Amelia Jane found if you look at the picture. She didn't know what it was, at first. Then, when she threw it into the air and found that it came back to her, she was thrilled.

'Now I'll have some fun!' she cried, and she threw the boomerang at the chimneys on the dolls' house! It knocked them off and they slid down the roof, fell to the ground and gave the clockwork mouse a terrible fright.

The boomerang flew back to Amelia Jane, and she caught it. 'Now I'll take off the sailor doll's hat!' she said with a giggle, and threw it again. It neatly took off the sailor doll's hat, and came back to Amelia Jane. She laughed at the sailor doll's look of surprise when he felt his hat knocked off.

'Oh, my goodness! Amelia Jane has found the old boomerang!' said the bear. 'I hid it away. Amelia, give it to me.'

Amelia Jane threw the boomerang at him,

and it sliced off the tip of one of his ears, and then flew back to the doll. The bear was very angry.

He ran at Amelia to get the boomerang. But she flung it at him again and he fell over. The boomerang returned to her hand. She laughed excitedly.

'It's no good! I'm *awfully* good with this. If you come rushing at me I'll throw it at you. So keep away. Now watch – I'm going to throw it at the snapdragons in that vase! I'll chop off some of their heads!'

And that's just what she did! The boomerang flew through the air, hit two snapdragons, broke their pretty heads, and then came flying back to the naughty doll.

Amelia Jane had a lovely time that day. She knocked the little china dog off the

mantelpiece with her boomerang and he fell on to the hearth and broke a bit off one paw. She threw it at the little mouse who came for crumbs, and he lost two of his whiskers. And she threw it at the railway train and cut the funnel right off.

'How can we stop it?' said the clockwork clown in despair. He had had his hat knocked off six times by the boomerang and now he had stuffed it into his pocket for safety.

'I know where the old pop-gun is,' said the pink cat suddenly. 'Shall we get that? It's got a cork on a string, and it always jerks back when it's shot out. You put the cork into the end of the gun, press the trigger – and out shoots the cork. But because it's on a string it always jerks back to the shooter again, like the boomerang goes back to Amelia Jane.'

※ 226 ※

This was quite a long speech for the pink cat to make, and everyone listened to it, except Amelia Jane, who was trying to knock down a silver thimble left on the mantelpiece.

'Yes! Get the pop-gun!' cried the bear, so the pink cat went to get it. He brought it out of an old box and showed it to the others. Tom the toy soldier fitted the cork into the end. It was on a long string tied to the gun.

He pressed the trigger.

POP! Out flew the cork quite fiercely, and hit the bear on the right paw. He gave a yell. 'Don't practise on me, silly! That stung! Practise on Amelia Jane!'

Tom grinned. He went over to Amelia Jane and pointed the pop-gun at the back of her head.

POP! The cork flew out, caught her hair-ribbon, and then jerked back on its string.

Amelia Jane got a terrible shock.

'Oh! What was that?' she cried, and swung round at once.

'We've got a boomerang-cork!' grinned Tom, and shot at her again. POP! The cork hit her on the nose, and she almost fell over.

'Now you stop that!' cried Amelia Jane,

'or I'll throw my boomerang at you!'

'Well, every time you throw your boomerang we're going to shoot you with the pop-gun!' said Tom, putting the cork into the gun again. 'There's no reason why we shouldn't have a bit of fun, too! Look out!'

Pop! The cork hit Amelia Jane right in her middle and she gave a squeal. 'Oh! Oh! You've hit my dinner! Wait till I get that horrid cork! I'll throw it away!'

But she couldn't get the cork because it was tied on with string to the gun, and it always jerked back when it was fired out.

The toys had a wonderful time chasing her round the nursery, popping the cork at her. She didn't have a chance to throw the boomerang at them.

'You're very unkind,' she sobbed as she tried to dodge the toys.

'Oh, no – we're only doing the sort of thing you've been doing,' said Tom. 'You give us your boomerang and we'll give you the pop-gun. Then we can each have a turn at throwing the boomerang too.'

'No,' said Amelia. 'You'd only throw that at me as well. Promise not to and I'll give it to you.'

They promised, and Amelia Jane handed over the boomerang. Tom at once went to hide it away where it would never be found again. But, oh dear, Amelia Jane didn't promise not to shoot at the toys with the pop-gun, and the very first thing she did was to point it at the bear and fire.

POP! It flew out and hit him so hard in his

tummy that it made him growl. But she couldn't shoot the cork again because Tom had cut the string and it didn't jerk back to the gun!

'Aha!' said the sailor doll, picking up the loose cork and putting it into his pocket, 'you won't do *that* again, naughty Amelia Jane! Go and stand in the corner till we say you can come out. If you don't, we'll take the gun, tie on the string to the cork and do a bit of shooting again!'

So Amelia Jane is standing in the corner, sulking, and I rather think the toys are going to forget about her for a very long time!

Amelia Jane and the Scribbles

One day Amelia Jane found a red pencil on the floor. Somebody had dropped it there and forgotten to pick it up. Amelia Jane was pleased.

'Now I can write things in red,' she said. 'Look, this is a pencil that writes in red, toys.'

'Well, if you think you're going to write in my notebook, you're wrong,' said Tom.

'And if you think I'm going to lend you my little drawing-book to scribble in, you can think again,' said the teddy bear.

'And don't you dare to scribble inside the lid of the brick-box,' said the clockwork clown. 'I spent ages rubbing out some silly scribbles the pink cat did once with a bit of coal.'

'I don't know why you're so sharp with me,' said Amelia Jane. 'Anyone would think I wanted to do something naughty.'

'It's not at all surprising that we should think that,' said the bear. 'You've been fairly good for about a week. That's about as long as you *can* be good for.'

Amelia Jane badly wanted to scribble with her red pencil, but nobody would lend her any paper at all. So she got cross and went inside the toy-cupboard all by herself. When she came out, she was smiling.

'Now, what's she smiling like that for?' said Tom, and he went inside the toy-cupboard. He gave an angry cry, and the toys went to see why.

'Look!' he said, pointing to the wall at the back of the cupboard. 'Look what she's done.'

The toys looked. Written across the wall were lots of words: '*The toy soldier is silly. The teddy bear is too fat. The clockwork clown is clumsy. The clockwork mouse is a baby.*'

'Look at that!' said the clown. 'How disgraceful! Doesn't Amelia Jane know that

no decent people ever scribble on walls? Only
the very lowest toys do that!'

They went to find Amelia, but they
couldn't. But they found something scribbled
on the wall near the toy-cupboard, at the
bottom:

'You're all sillies! I shall do what I like, so there! Signed, Amelia Jane.'

'Isn't she awful?' said the bear. 'Now we shall have to spend ages rubbing this out before anyone sees it. Go and borrow some dusters from the dolls in the dolls' house, Tom.'

But when he got to the dolls' house, he found all the small dolls in a very bad temper.

'Somebody's been in and scribbled over our walls,' said Dinah, the mother doll. 'Look. Someone's written: "*This is a silly dolls' house!*".'

'What a shame,' said the bear. 'That's Amelia Jane. She wants scribbling on herself!'

'That's an awfully good idea of yours, bear,' said the clown. 'If only we could! That would soon stop her silly tricks!'

'Listen,' said the bear, thinking out a plan. 'We're giving a party tomorrow night, aren't we, to all the pixies who live in the garden outside? Well, let's wait till Amelia Jane is asleep tonight, and we'll scribble something across her forehead! She won't know, because she hardly ever looks at herself in the mirror, even to do her hair.'

All the toys giggled. That would be a good joke! They spent quite a lot of time rubbing out the things Amelia Jane had scribbled everywhere, and the big doll peeped out from behind the curtain, and laughed. She didn't know what they were planning for her, or she would have been on her guard.

That night Amelia Jane climbed up into one of the dolls' cots and lay down to sleep. She felt tired. She had done such a lot of writing that day! The toys waited till she was fast asleep, and then Tom climbed up softly to the cot. He sat down gently beside Amelia Jane.

'Pass me the paintbox,' he whispered, and the bear passed it up. A bright red colour was already mixed for him, and the paintbrush was there as well.

Tom began to paint words quickly on Amelia Jane's big smooth forehead. '*This is naughty Amelia Jane*' he put, and tried not to giggle.

Amelia Jane thought it was a fly walking over her head when she felt the paintbrush in her sleep. 'Go away, fly,' she murmured, and that made Tom almost laugh out loud.

He slid down to the floor when he had finished. He wouldn't let the others go up and see what he had done, in case they wakened Amelia Jane. 'Wait till she wakes,' he said. 'Oh, won't it be funny at the party? We shan't need to introduce Amelia Jane to anyone! They'll only have to read what's on her forehead!'

Well, it *was* funny! The pixie guests came along in crowds, longing to dance to the music of the musical-box and to eat the little cakes that Dinah had cooked on the dolls'-house stove. The bear was the host, and he introduced everyone.

But he didn't need to say who Amelia Jane was because as soon as the guests saw her they all giggled and said: 'Oh, this is naughty Amelia Jane!'

Amelia Jane was surprised and cross. She didn't like being called naughty at a party. She frowned and sulked. But as soon as everyone came up to her, the same thing was said: 'Oh, this is naughty Amelia Jane!'

'Why do you say that?' said Amelia, crossly, and she frowned so hard that she wrinkled up all the red words on her forehead.

'Don't do that – we can't read your name!' said a small pixie. Amelia Jane stared at him.

'What do you mean, you can't read my name? Of course you can't. Don't be silly.'

'Oh, now I can,' said the little pixie, when Amelia had stopped frowning. 'Yes – this is naughty Amelia Jane.'

Amelia Jane went to the teddy bear, almost crying. 'Why is everyone horrid to me? Why do they keep saying, "This is naughty Amelia Jane"? Tell me.'

'No,' said the bear.

'Yes,' said Amelia. 'I want to know, please, please, bear.'

'I'll tell you if you promise to give me that red pencil and never to scribble anywhere again,' said the bear. 'It's a low thing to do.'

'All right,' said Amelia Jane, with a sigh. 'I won't scribble anymore. Here's the pencil.'

'Thanks. Now go and look at yourself in the mirror,' said the bear, and Amelia went.

She screamed when she saw the red words

on her forehead. 'Oh! Oh, how mean! Now I know why everyone said what they did. I shan't go back to the party.'

So she didn't. She stayed and moped in the toy-cupboard, and that's where the bear found her halfway through. 'Come along,' he said. 'Come and dance.'

'No,' said Amelia. 'Not with this horrid scribble on my forehead.'

The bear took out his hanky. 'Lick it,' he said to Amelia Jane, and she licked his hanky. He rubbed the licky bit over her forehead.

'There!' he said. 'The scribble's gone. Now come along and dance – and mind you behave yourself, or I might write something else on you. You never know!'

So Amelia Jane behaved herself. But I'm afraid her good behaviour won't last long!

Amelia Jane Plays Postman

I really must tell you the latest story about
Amelia Jane.

On the nursery mantelpiece stood a
money-box. It looked exactly like a pillar
box, and it was painted red just like the big
ones we post letters in down the road.

But instead of posting letters in their box the
children posted money, of course, and it was
a very good way of saving it. 'Clink!' it went
when it was dropped in, and the money-box
grew heavier and heavier.

Mother kept the key of the box and only
unlocked it when the children wanted to take
out some money to buy someone a birthday

present. She unlocked the box at the bottom then, and the children took the money out.

Now, Amelia Jane suddenly took it into her head that if she found anything left about by the toys she would post it in the red money-box on the mantelpiece! That made the toys very angry indeed.

'Amelia Jane! Have you taken my pink ribbon?' cried the bear.

'Yes. And I've posted it,' said Amelia. 'You are getting very untidy, Teddy, leaving your things about. It will teach you to be tidy.'

Teddy was furious, of course. And so was the clockwork clown when he found that Amelia had actually posted the button that came off his trousers.

'How dare you do that?' he shouted. 'I couldn't help it coming off, could I? I know somebody would have sewn it on again, if you hadn't picked it up and posted it. You're SILLY, Amelia Jane!'

And then she posted the toy soldier's belt! It was a bit tight, so he had undone it and had just put it down while he straightened his trousers a little, when Amelia Jane pounced on it. He was too late to get it back! Into the red money-box it went.

'Now I haven't got a belt!' shouted Tom. 'I look awful. Stop this nonsense, Amelia Jane, or we'll start posting *your* things in that box!'

'You can't,' said Amelia with a grin. 'I'm the only one that can reach the mantelpiece.'

This was quite true. Amelia Jane was a very big doll and a good climber too. She could reach up to the chair near the fireplace, climb over to the mantelpiece and climb on to that. Then it was easy to post anything in the money-box there.

But none of the other toys could get on to the mantelpiece, so they couldn't possibly post anything belonging to Amelia. It was most annoying. After she had posted the baby doll's dear little comb, the toys held a meeting. Amelia Jane was asleep in her chair, so she didn't hear a word.

❀ 251 ❀

'We've got to do *some*thing to stop her,' said the clock. 'She'll be posting the clockwork mouse's tail next!'

The mouse gave a squeal. 'No, no! Don't say that! I couldn't bear it.'

'How can we stop her?' wondered the baby doll.

The teddy bear suddenly slapped his plump knee.

'I know. I've got an idea!'

'Sh! Don't wake Amelia,' said the clown.

'Now listen,' said the teddy, excitedly. 'You know next week it's the birthday of the little mouse who lives in the hole in the wall, don't you? Well, listen – ooooh, it's *such* a good idea – you see . . .'

'Oh, do go on! Do tell us!' said the clockwork mouse, impatiently.

'Well – we'll pretend that we are giving the little mouse all sorts of tiny presents, wrapped up in parcels,' said the teddy, grinning. '*But* – we'll put inside the parcels little things belonging to Amelia Jane! We'll put her best hair-ribbon in – and one of her Sunday shoes – and that brooch she likes so much – and her best sash . . .'

'But dear me, we can't *possibly* give her things to the little mouse,' said Tom, shocked. 'That would be quite wrong.'

'Oh, don't you *see* what will happen?' said the teddy. 'Amelia Jane will find the parcels – and she won't be able to stop herself *posting* them – in the money-box! And she'll have posted all her own things and won't be able to get them back!'

There was a silence. Then the toys giggled

and thumped Teddy on the back. 'You're marvellous!' they cried. 'It is a simply wonderful idea! We'll do it! Oh, how we'll laugh to see Amelia posting her own things!'

Well, they did just what they had planned.

They found Amelia's brooch and wrapped it up. They found her best sash, folded it neatly and wrapped it in paper and tied it with string. They took her hair-ribbon and did that up too, and one of her best shoes! Soon there were four neat little parcels at the back of the toy-cupboard.

And, of course, it wasn't long before Amelia Jane found them. 'Aha!' she said. 'I suppose these are birthday parcels for that silly little mouse who lives in the wall. I'll post them!'

'I warn you not to,' said Tom. 'You'll be sorry if you do, Amelia.'

Amelia laughed and picked up all the parcels. She went towards the fireplace to climb on the chair there.

'You have been warned!' called the clown. But Amelia took no notice at all. Ha – this was a fine trick to play on the toys – to post all the parcels they had got ready for the little mouse!

Thud, thud, thud, thud! Down into the money-box they went, and there they stayed. Amelia Jane climbed down, smiling. 'I have been warned!' she said, mockingly. 'But *I* don't care.'

Nobody said anything. They just waited in patience till Amelia wanted her brooch or her ribbon or sash. She soon did, because she was to go to a party given by the doll in the next house. The children were taking her.

'I shall wear my best shoes, my sash, my blue hair-ribbon, and my brooch,' she said. 'I *shall* look grand!'

But she couldn't find them, though she hunted everywhere. She turned to the watching toys. 'You know something about them!' she cried. 'What have you done with them?'

'Nothing – except just wrap them up into neat little parcels!' grinned the clown.

'But what for? Oh, *what's* happened to my precious, precious things?' groaned Amelia.

'You should know,' said the bear. 'You picked up all the parcels yesterday.'

'You p-p-p-posted them!' squealed the clockwork mouse, stammering in excitement, and then going off into a fit of giggles.

'I *posted* them!' said Amelia. 'What do you mean? Those were birthday parcels for the mouse, weren't they? Oh, oh, oh – why didn't you tell me what they were?'

'We warned you, we did warn you not to post them,' said the clown, and he went off into giggles, too.

Amelia Jane cried bitterly. She didn't go to the party. She moped all day long till the toys felt quite sorry for her. Then she dried her eyes.

'I'm sorry I posted everybody's things,' she said. 'I know what it feels like now to lose my things in that money-box. I'll find the key, undo the box and get everything out.'

But she couldn't find the key because Mother had it in her purse. So everything has got to stay there till somebody has a birthday and the money-box is unlocked.

And *what* a surprise the children are going to get when they see all the things that Amelia Jane has posted! I'm sure the clockwork mouse will have a fit of the giggles again!

Amelia Jane is Naughty Again

Listen to what Amelia Jane did a little while ago – she's almost as rascally as Brer Rabbit sometimes!

It all happened when a new toy came to stay in the nursery. He really belonged to the children's cousin, but she was going away and asked her cousins to look after this toy for her.

He was rather a peculiar-looking toy. He was made of wood, and he had jointed legs and arms and hands – and even toes. He was dressed like a gardener, with a green baize apron in front, a scarf round his neck, and rolled-up sleeves that showed his jointed arms.

The peculiar thing about him was his head. It could nod up and down and shake from side to side because it was on a kind of spring.

It was very surprising to the toys to see somebody that could nod his head or shake it like that.

'What's your name?' asked Amelia Jane. 'Do we call you Mr Noddy or Mr Shaky?'

'I've got a cousin called Mr Shaky,' said the wooden man. 'I'm called Mr Up-and-To.'

'What a peculiar name!' said the sailor doll.

'Not really,' said the wooden man. 'Just a mixture of *Up*-and-Down and *To*-and-Fro – Mr Up-and-To.'

'Why not Mr Fro-and-Down?' asked Amelia Jane, and went off into giggles.

'How clever you are!' said Mr Up-and-To, admiringly. 'That's a *much* nicer name! Really, I think you are a very clever doll.'

'Oh, I am,' said Amelia Jane at once. 'Aren't I, toys? If anything goes wrong, ask me how to put it right! If you want to know anything, ask me! If you –'

'That's enough, Amelia Jane,' said Tom. 'Stop blowing your own trumpet.'

'Oh, can she blow a trumpet, too?' said Mr Up-and-To, surprised. 'Well, well – if that isn't cleverer still. My mouth's too wooden to hold a trumpet.'

'Amelia's mouth is big enough to hold a dozen trumpets, if she wanted to blow them about herself,' said the bear.

'Don't be unkind,' said Amelia Jane. 'You know I'm very clever.'

'I know you're very, very naughty,' said the bear. 'Now, you leave Mr Up-and-To alone, and don't stuff him up with any more tales.'

But Amelia Jane wouldn't leave the little wooden man alone. For one thing, he really was very, very stupid, and he believed every word anyone said. Amelia Jane found that out at once, and, oh, the tricks she played on that poor wooden man!

'Don't go near the brick-box,' she would say. 'It's Monday today, and there might be a snake there!'

And, will you believe it, Mr Up-and-To would keep right the other side of the nursery, afraid that a snake might spring out at him.

'Don't go too near the Noah's Ark today, because it's Friday,' Amelia would say next. 'The lions are always so fierce on Friday.'

Mr Up-and-To didn't go near the Noah's Ark all day long. He asked Amelia Jane why the lions were so fierce on Fridays.

'Well, I expect that's the day they're fed at the Zoo,' said Amelia Jane, and the poor stupid little wooden man thought that was a very good reason.

'You're bad, Amelia Jane,' said Tom. 'Stuffing him up with tales like that. Whatever will you say next?'

'Aha! You wait and see!' said Amelia. And she went and whispered in Mr Up-and-To's big wooden ear.

'Don't go near the toy soldier today
because it's Saturday and he might bite you.'

Poor Mr Up-and-To! He ran away as soon
as Tom came near, and as Amelia Jane had
given Tom a sweet to take to the wooden
man, he kept on trying to find him, so that he
could give him the sweet.

'I can't *think* why the wooden man keeps
rushing off as soon as he sees me,' said Tom,
surprised.

'It's Saturday and he doesn't like soldiers on
Saturday,' said Amelia Jane, wickedly.

'Don't be silly,' said Tom. 'Here, take your
sweet back. I'm not going to rush after Mr
Up-and-To all day long. You've told him
something about me. I know you!'

Now one day Amelia Jane put a knot into

her little blue hanky to remind her not to forget to mend her dress. Mr Up-and-To saw her knotting the knot, and he was most interested.

'What's that for?' he asked.

'Well, most people put a knot into their hanky if they want to remember something,' said Amelia. 'This knot says to me: "Mend your dress tonight, Amelia Jane." And I shall.'

'Very, very clever,' said the wooden man. 'I think I shall do that too, Amelia. I'm always forgetting things, aren't I?'

'Well, you just try putting knots into your hanky, and you will soon have a marvellous memory,' said Amelia Jane.

So the next time Mr Up-and-To wanted to remember something, he took out his big, red-spotted hanky and tied a very large knot in it.

'That's to tell me to remember to clean my shoes tonight,' he said to himself. But, of course, when he saw the knot again he couldn't for the life of him remember what he had put it into his hanky for.

I'll ask Amelia Jane, he thought. She always knows everything. So he went to find the big doll.

'Amelia,' he said, 'supposing I forgot what I had put a knot in my hanky for, would you be able to tell me?'

'Of course!' said Amelia, with a very wicked grin.

'Well, what's this knot for?' asked the wooden man, and he showed her the very big knot.

'Oh – that's to remind you to climb up to the basin-taps with a jug from the dolls'

house, fill it with water, and give me a drink,' said Amelia at once.

'Is it really?' said the wooden man, in surprise. 'Well, fancy me forgetting that! I'll go at once, Amelia Jane.'

So, much to the toys' amazement, he got a jug, climbed all the way up to the basin, and held the jug under the tap-drips till he got it full. Then he gave Amelia Jane a drink.

'Well! He must be very fond of her,' said the clockwork clown, in surprise. 'Fancy doing all that for *Amelia*!'

Amelia was pleased. Her naughty mind began to work hard – and the very next time Mr Up-and-To was asleep she crept up to him, took his hanky from his pocket and made a very big knot there!

So, of course, the next time he took it out

another knot stared him in the face. What *could* it be for?

'Oh, that?' said Amelia Jane. 'Dear, dear, have you forgotten already why you put it there, Mr Up-and-To? Why, it was to remind you to go to the toy sweet shop and bring me six of those tiny pink sweets.'

'Dear me – was it really?' said Mr Up-and-To, puzzled. 'I simply can't remember that at all! But I'll go at once, Amelia Jane.'

So he solemnly went to the toy-shop and took six of the little pink sweets from a bottle and gave them to Amelia Jane. She popped them all into her mouth at once.

Tom and the bear came over in a hurry. They spoke very sternly to Mr Up-and-To.

'Look here! That's stealing. Those sweets belong to the children, not to us. How dare you! Put them back!'

'He can't,' said Amelia, speaking with her mouth full. 'I'm eating them.'

'Did she tell you to get them?' the bear asked the wooden man.

'Well, no – not exactly. I – er – I put a knot in my hanky to remember to get them,' said Mr Up-and-To. 'I must say I'm very surprised at myself for putting a knot there to remind me of that. I'm very, very sorry, Teddy.'

Amelia Jane giggled to herself. She felt very naughty indeed, with a nice stupid fellow like Mr Up-and-To to play tricks on.

She put more knots in his hanky, and when he asked her what they could possibly be for she told him all sorts of things.

'That knot you put there is to remind you to get me the little blue brooch you'll find in a box at the back of the toy-cupboard,' she said. It belonged to the baby doll, and it was very bad of Amelia Jane to get the wooden man to fetch it for her.

'And that knot's to remind you to get me some cakes from the dolls'-house kitchen,' said Amelia another time. 'They've been baking today. And look, there's a little tiny knot in this corner of your hanky – that's to tell you to remember to have a cake for yourself, too.'

And, dear me, there were Amelia Jane and the wooden man both eating cakes together!

The toys were very, very angry, and the dolls'-house dolls threatened to fetch a policeman.

'If you tell Mr Up-and-To any more naughty things to do, we'll punish you,

Amelia Jane,' said the bear. 'Oh, we know
it's you all right! He's too stupid to think of
these things himself. You put them into his
head.'

Amelia got cross. She put *four* knots in
Mr Up-and-To's hanky at once. He ran to
her, most surprised, when he discovered them.

'Amelia Jane! Look here – I've put *four* knots this time. Whatever can they be for?'

'This one's to remind you to pull the toy soldier's nose, and this one's to remind you to tread on the tail of the clockwork mouse, and that's to tell you to be sure and pinch the teddy bear, and that's to remind you to run off with the clown's key,' said Amelia Jane.

Well, the wooden man was most astonished at himself. To think he had decided to do all those things and had actually put knots in his hanky to remind him. Well, well – he'd better start off with the toy soldier. He would pull his nose.

He tried to, but Tom caught his wooden hands, and stopped him.

'Listen, Mr Up-and-To,' he said sternly. 'What's up with you? You *seem* so gentle and good, and a bit stupid – and yet you do all kinds of very, very naughty things. Why?'

'It's the knots in my hanky,' explained the wooden man sadly. 'Amelia Jane always tells me what they're for, you see. She knows.'

The toys went off to the back of the toy-cupboard to have a meeting. So *that's* what

Amelia Jane was doing!

'She puts the knots in the hanky when the old wooden man is asleep,' said Teddy. 'And then when he asks her what he's put them there for, she tells him all kinds of nonsense. Well – *I'm* going to tell him what his next knot is for!'

The toys grinned. They could guess what the bear was going to tell Mr Up-and-To.

It was the bear that night who put a knot into the wooden man's hanky. It was such an enormous knot that the hanky seemed all knot when he had finished!

Mr Up-and-To was astonished to see such a big knot when he woke up. The bear was just nearby, so instead of asking Amelia Jane he showed the knot to Teddy.

'Look at that!' he said. 'A tremendous knot.

Something *most* important to remember. I'd better ask Amelia Jane what it is for.'

'No, don't,' said the bear. 'She wouldn't dream of telling you what the knot's for. Ask me – or the toy soldier – or the clown. We all know. We'll tell you all right.'

'Tell me then,' said the wooden man.

'That knot, that very large knot, is to remind you to be sure and give Amelia Jane a good scolding,' said the bear. 'Don't look so surprised. That's what the knot is there for. Isn't it, Tom? Isn't it, everyone?'

And all the toys nodded and said yes, that was what the very large knot meant.

'She's been bad to you,' said Teddy. 'She's tried to make you bad, too. She must be punished – and you are the one to punish her, Mr Up-and-To. Go now.'

So he's gone to find Amelia Jane, feeling very cross indeed. She tried to make him bad, did she? Mr Up-and-To didn't want to be bad. He'd give Amelia Jane a good scolding!

She's hiding, of course. But the wooden man will find her. He's very, very determined once he makes his mind up – and sooner or later there'll be howls from the nursery, I'm sure of that.

I don't feel a bit sorry, and neither does anyone else. Amelia Jane has had her fun, and now, alas, she's got to pay for it!

Amelia Jane Goes up the Tree

It was springtime, and the birds were all nesting. Amelia Jane was most excited.

'The birds are building their nests,' she said. 'They are laying eggs.'

'Well, they do that every year,' said Tom.

'I want to make a collection of birds' eggs,' said Amelia Jane, grandly.

'You naughty doll!' said the clockwork clown. 'You know quite well you mustn't take birds' eggs.'

'Well, I don't see why birds can't spare me one or two of their eggs,' said Amelia. 'After all – they can't count.'

'Amelia Jane, you know quite well that
birds get dreadfully upset if they see anyone
near their nests,' said the teddy bear. 'You
know that sometimes they get very
frightened, and they desert their nests – leave
them altogether – so that the eggs get cold,
and never hatch out.'

'Oh, don't lecture me so!' said Amelia Jane. 'I said I wanted to make a collection of birds' eggs, and so I am going to. You can't stop me.'

'You are a very bad doll,' said the clown, and he turned his back on Amelia. 'I don't like you one bit.'

Amelia Jane laughed. She was feeling in a very naughty mood. She looked out of the window, down into a big chestnut tree. In the fork of a branch was a nest. It belonged to a thrush.

'There's a thrush's nest just down there,' said Amelia. 'I wish I could climb down. But I can't. It's too dangerous. Perhaps I could climb up.'

'How could you do that?' said the curly-haired doll, in a scornful voice. 'Don't be silly.

None of us could climb up that tall trunk!'

But the next day Amelia Jane was excited. 'The gardener has put a ladder up the chestnut tree!' she said. 'He has, really. He is cutting off some of the bigger branches, because they knock against the low roof of the shed. I shall slip down, wait till the gardener has gone to his dinner, and then climb the ladder!'

'Amelia Jane! You don't mean to say you really *are* going to rob a bird's nest!' cried the clown.

'Oh yes,' said Amelia. 'Why should the bird mind if one or two eggs are taken? She will probably be glad that she hasn't so many hungry beaks to fill, when the eggs hatch out!'

So, to the horror of the watching toys,

Amelia Jane slipped downstairs, out of the garden door and up to the ladder, as soon as the gardener had gone to his dinner.

The toys all pressed their noses to the window and watched her.

'She's climbing the ladder!' said the clown. 'She really is!'

'She's up to the top of it!' squeaked the clockwork mouse.

'She's going right into the tree!' cried the teddy bear, and he almost broke the window with his nose, he pressed so hard against it.

Amelia Jane was climbing the tree very well. She was a big strong doll, and she swung herself up easily. She soon came to the big thrush's nest. The mother-thrush was not there.

I suppose she has gone to stretch her wings

a little, thought Amelia Jane. She stretched out her hand and put it into the nest. There were four eggs there, and they felt smooth and warm. Amelia Jane took one and put it into the pocket of her red dress. Then she took another, and put that in her second pocket.

'There!' she said. 'Two will be enough, I think. I can start a very nice collection with two. How pretty they are! I like them.'

She sat up in the tree for a little while, enjoying the sound of the wind in the leaves and liking the swaying of the bough she sat on. It was so exciting.

'I'd better go back now,' she said. 'I don't want to be here when the mother-thrush comes back.'

So she began to climb down the tree again.

But, after a while, she heard a noise. It was someone whistling. She peeped down between the leaves.

'It's the gardener!' said Amelia Jane in dismay. 'Oh dear, I hope he isn't coming up the tree now.'

He wasn't. He was doing something else – something that filled Amelia Jane with great dismay.

'He's taking away the ladder! Oh my! It's gone! However am I to get down again? The ladder's gone!'

It certainly *was* gone. The gardener, still whistling, carried it away for another job. And there was Amelia Jane, left high up the tree!

She sat there for a long time. She heard the thrush come back again to her nest.

She heard the wind in the trees. She saw the toys in the nursery looking out at her in surprise, wondering why she didn't climb down and come back.

'I do feel lonely and frightened,' said Amelia to herself, when the day went and the cold night began to come. 'I shall be very afraid up here in the dark. Oh dear, why ever did I think of climbing the tree and stealing eggs? It's a punishment for me, it really is!'

She began to cry. And when Amelia Jane cried she made a noise. She sobbed and gulped and howled. It was a dreadful noise.

A small pixie, who lived in the primrose bed below, heard the noise and wondered what it was. So she flew up into the tree to see.

'Oh, it's you, Amelia Jane,' said the pixie. 'What's the matter? You're keeping me

awake with that dreadful noise.'

'I can't get down,' sobbed Amelia. 'I want to get back to the nursery, and I can't.'

'Whatever made you climb up?' asked the pixie. But Amelia was too ashamed to tell her.

'Please help me,' begged the big doll. 'I am so unhappy.'

'Well, maybe the thrush who lives higher up the tree can help you,' said the pixie, and she flew up to see. Amelia Jane felt most uncomfortable. She had taken eggs from the thrush's nest. Oh dear! How she wished she hadn't!

The pixie flew back again, and the big brown thrush was with her.

'Here's the thrush,' said the pixie. 'She is very sad and unhappy tonight, because some horrid person stole two of her precious eggs, but she is very kind, and although she is sad she will help you.'

'Yes, I will help you, help you, help you,' sang the thrush sweetly. 'I am sad, sad, sad, but I will help you, big, big doll.'

'How can you help me?' asked Amelia in surprise.

'I can guide you right up the tree,' said the thrush. 'I know the way. I can bring you right up to the nursery window-sill, and you can knock on the window and get the toys to let you in. Then you will be safe, safe, safe!'

'Oh, you *are* kind!' said Amelia Jane. She turned to follow the thrush up the tree.

'Hold on to one of my tail-feathers,' said the thrush kindly. 'Don't be afraid of pulling it out.'

Amelia held on to a feather, and the thrush guided her gently up the dark tree. After a little while she stopped and spoke.

'Big doll, can you see my nest just here? It is such a nice, comfortable one. It is very dark now, but perhaps you can just see two eggs gleaming in the cup. Aren't they lovely?'

Amelia Jane could see them gleaming in the half-darkness. The thrush went on, half speaking, half singing.

'You know, I had more eggs than those you see. But whilst I was away this morning someone took two, took two, took two. It nearly broke my heart. Now I shall only have two children instead of four. Can you imagine anyone bad enough to steal from a little bird like me?'

Amelia Jane felt the two eggs in her pockets, and she began to sob. 'What's the matter?' asked the kindly thrush; and she pressed her warm, feathery body close to Amelia to comfort her.

'Oh, brown thrush, oh, brown thrush,' sobbed Amelia. 'I took your eggs. I've got them in my pockets. Let me put them back into your nest, please, please! They are still lovely and warm, and I haven't broken them. I'm the horrid person that took them, but I'm dreadfully sorry now!'

She took the warm eggs from her pockets and put them gently into the nest.

'Now push me down the tree; do anything you like to punish me!' said Amelia Jane. 'I know I deserve it.'

'What a foolish doll you are!' said the thrush, very happy to see her eggs once more. 'Because you were unkind to me is no reason why I should now be unkind to you. I am happy again, so I want to make you happy, too! Come along, hold on to my tail-feather, and we'll go higher till we come to the window-sill!'

So up they went, with Amelia wiping her

eyes on her skirt every now and again because she was so ashamed of herself and so grateful to the thrush for forgiving her and being kind to her.

They came to the window-sill, and Amelia rapped on it. The teddy bear, who was just the other side, called the clown, and together they opened the window. Amelia slipped inside. She said goodbye to the thrush, and then looked at the toys.

'Whatever happened to you?' said the clown. 'Did you take the eggs? Surely that was the thrush helping you just now!'

'I did take the eggs, but I've given them back, and I'm ashamed of myself for taking them,' said Amelia in a very small voice. 'I shall never, never do such a thing again in my life. I'm going to be a Good Doll now.'

'Hmmm,' said the clown. 'We've heard that before, Amelia Jane! We'll see what the thrush has to say tomorrow!'

I heard her singing the next day, and do you know what she sang? She sang: 'Took two, took two, put them back, put them back, put them back, sweet, sweet, sweet!' Listen, and maybe you'll hear her singing that, too!

Amelia Jane
Gets Into Trouble

Contents

Amelia Jane and
the Telephone

There was a new toy in the nursery. It was
a little telephone. It stood on the nursery
bookshelf looking exactly like a real one,
but much smaller.

The toys didn't dare to touch it. They were
afraid of the real telephone, and they were
afraid of the toy one, too.

Outside in the passage they often heard the
bell of the real telephone ringing loudly, and
it made them jump. Then someone would
come along, take the receiver off the
telephone and speak into it.

'Hallo!' they would say. 'Hallo!' And then

they would speak to somebody far, far away, and it all seemed very like magic.

Amelia Jane, the big naughty doll, had been away for a few days. When she came back the first thing she saw was the toy telephone.

'Aha!' she said, and went over to it. 'A telephone. Good. We need one in the nursery.'

'Don't touch it, Amelia Jane – a telephone is very magic,' cried Tom the toy soldier. 'Voices come into it, you know – people who are far, far away can speak to you. Be careful, in case somebody's voice is in that toy telephone now!'

'Pooh!' said Amelia Jane. 'I'm just going to do a bit of ordering – like Mother does sometimes on the real telephone out in the passage.'

And, to the toys' horror, she picked up the little receiver, put one end to her ear, and spoke into the other end.

'Is that the butcher? Send four sausages to the nursery, please. Is that the baker?

Send four buns to the nursery, please. Is that the watchmaker? Send one nice new watch to the nursery, please – and, oh, please see that the letters A. J. are on the back. A. J. for Amelia Jane. Thank you.' She put back the receiver and smiled round at the astonished toys. 'There you are! I've done a nice little bit of ordering. We'll enjoy the sausages and the buns. We can divide them up between us. And I always wanted a watch.'

Of course, Amelia Jane knew quite well that she hadn't been speaking to the butcher, the baker and the watchmaker. She was just making the toys think she was very daring and grand.

But the toys were really very worried. They climbed up to the windowsill to watch for the goods to arrive.

'The thing is – how are we to pay for them?' said the teddy bear. 'I haven't got any money!'

'I've got a penny that I found under the carpet,' said the clockwork mouse.

'Shall we be put into prison if we order things we can't pay for?' asked the clockwork clown.

Nobody knew – but they thought it was very likely. Tom the toy soldier went to Amelia Jane.

'Please, Amelia Jane, ring up the butcher, the baker and the watchmaker and tell them not to send the things after all,' he said.

'What will you give me if I do?' asked Amelia Jane at once.

'Oh dear – I'll give you my best hanky,' said Tom. 'And the mouse will give you his penny. Have *you* got anything to give, Teddy?'

'Just a good scolding,' said the teddy, rather fiercely. 'I'll give that with pleasure.'

'Give me the hanky and the money, and I'll ring up the butcher, the baker and the watchmaker,' said

Amelia Jane. So they gave her them, and she went to the telephone.

'I haven't given you my scolding,' said the bear, but Amelia took no notice. She spoke into the telephone:

'Is that the butcher? We don't want the

sausages after all. Is that the baker? We don't want the buns. Is that the watchmaker? I've changed my mind about the watch. Yes – yes. That's right. What's that? You want to send a message to the teddy bear? Oh, yes, of course, I'll give it to him.'

The toys were listening with all their ears. 'Right,' said Amelia, into the telephone. 'I'm to tell the bear he is a nasty, fat, tubby little creature, who can't even growl like a bear. Yes, certainly I'll tell him!'

'Don't you dare to tell me,' said the bear fiercely.

'All right, Teddy, I won't tell you that you are a nasty, fat, tubby little creature who can't even growl like a bear,' said Amelia Jane, annoyingly.

'But you *have* told him!' said Tom.

'No – I just told him what I wouldn't tell him,' said Amelia Jane.

She climbed up on to a shelf where nobody could reach her, not even the bear. She thought about the toy telephone. It would be very, very useful, she could see that. She would be able to make up all kinds of rude messages to pass on to the toys. She began to make a little plan.

Yes – she would invent somebody at the other end – somebody who would keep ringing up – and she would pretend to answer the telephone, and then give the horrid messages to all the toys. That would keep them in order all right!

She slipped down and went to the small toy bicycle that stood at one end of the nursery. It had a tiny little bell. She unscrewed it and put it into her pocket. She could ring it whenever she wanted to – and she would pretend it was the telephone bell ringing. That would make the toys jump!

The toys made up a song about Amelia Jane.

> *Amelia Jane*
> *Is naughty again,*
> *Let's go and leave her*
> *Out in the rain.*
> *Nobody loves her,*
> *Nobody cares*
> *If she gets eaten*
> *By lions or bears.*
> *She wants a scolding,*
> *It's perfectly plain;*
> *Amelia Jane,*
> *You are naughty again!*

Amelia listened to this song and felt very
angry indeed. How dare they sing that? Why,
even the clockwork mouse was singing and
waving his tail about in time to the tune.
Amelia walked over to the telephone and
sat down by it.

She put her hand into her pocket and rang

the little bell. It sounded just like the telephone bell suddenly ringing. The toys stopped singing in great surprise.

'The telephone rang!' they said to one another. 'Would you believe it? The telephone rang. Answer it, Amelia. See who wants to speak to us.'

Amelia picked up the receiver and put one end to her ear. 'Dear me – is that really Mr Mumbo-Jumbo?' she said, sounding astonished. 'This is Amelia Jane. What do you want, dear Mr Mumbo-Jumbo?'

The toys listened to this in amazement. Amelia Jane went on speaking. 'Yes, yes – I'll tell the bear. You're coming for him this evening, and you'll pull his nose for him till it's as long as an elephant's trunk. Yes, Mr Mumbo-Jumbo. Oh, yes – he is a bad bear. He deserves it. I'm sorry he was once so rude to you. Goodbye.'

She put down the receiver. The bear was trembling like a jelly, he was so scared.

'I was never rude to Mr Mumbo-Jumbo,' he wailed. 'I don't even know him. I never met him. I won't have my nose pulled, I won't, I won't.'

'I won't let you,' said Tom, comfortingly. 'I'll fight him.'

'So will I,' said the clockwork mouse, bravely. 'I'll nibble a hole in his leg.'

The telephone bell rang again – though, of course, it was only Amelia Jane putting her hand into her pocket and ringing the little bicycle bell. She picked up the receiver again and spoke into it.

'Hallo! Who's that? Oh, Mr Mumbo-Jumbo

again – what do you want this time, dear Mr
Mumbo-Jumbo? Yes, the clockwork mouse
lives here – and the toy soldier too. No, they
are not very nice toys. What am I to tell
them? You are coming tonight to catch the
toy soldier and peg him to your clothes-line?
And you're going to peg the clockwork mouse
up by his tail? Right, I'll tell them. Goodbye.'

'Oooooh!' squealed the clockwork mouse in
fright. 'He's not to come! I never did him any
harm!'

'Nor did I,' said Tom, turning pale. 'Who's
this awful fellow? He's not to come. I've
never been pegged up on a clothes-line in my
life, and nobody's going to do that to me.'

The bell rang again and Amelia Jane once
more spoke into the telephone. 'Oh – it's you,
Mr Mumbo-Jumbo, again. What's that?

You'll scold any toy who is rude to me? Thank you very much indeed. I'll tell you tonight who you can scold very severely!'

She made a rude face at the listening toys and went over to her cot. She climbed in. 'I'm going to have a good sleep,' she said. 'And anyone who disturbs me will be reported to Mr Mumbo-Jumbo!'

She shut her eyes and was soon fast asleep. She turned in her sleep – and out of her

pocket fell the little bicycle bell! The clockwork clown pounced on it.

'Look at that! She rang this when she

wanted us to think it was the telephone ringing! It was all a pretence on her part, the wicked doll. There wasn't any Mr Mumbo-Jumbo speaking to her over the telephone!'

'Let's wake her,' said Tom fiercely.

'No,' said the clown, speaking in a whisper. 'I've got a better idea. I know where there's a long piece of rubber tubing. I'll get it and fix it to the ear-piece of the telephone – and then, whoever speaks at the other end of the rubber tube can be heard in the telephone – *really* heard, not just pretending.'

'What's the use of that?' asked the bear.

'Wait and see,' said the clown. 'Now tonight one of us will ring this little bell, as if the telephone was ringing again – and Amelia can go and answer it – and Tom shall speak through the tube . . .'

'Oooooh, yes,' said everyone. 'That's a fine idea!'

'And he shall say, in a very dreadful voice: "This is Mr Mumbo-Jumbo speaking. Is that Amelia Jane? I've heard what a bad doll you are. And I'm coming to get you, Amelia. I'm walking up the passage now – I'm banging at the door. Let me in!"'

'But – what's the good of that?' said the bear. 'He won't come walking up and banging at the door.'

'Yes, he will,' grinned the clown. 'I shall be outside, listening – and *I'll* come stamping up the passage, and *I'll* bang hard at the door – see?'

'Amelia will think it's really Mr Mumbo-Jumbo out there and she'll be scared out of her life!' said the bear, chuckling. 'What a fine idea. Where's the rubber tube, clown?'

Well, before Amelia woke up, the rubber tubing was fixed to the telephone and run secretly into the toy-cupboard, where Tom was hiding. They all waited till Amelia awoke and stepped out of the cot.

At the same moment the bear, who was by the telephone, rang the little bell that had fallen from Amelia's pocket. 'R-r-r-r-ring!'

Amelia jumped and looked surprised. But she walked over to the telephone and took off the receiver, meaning to make up some more messages from Mumbo-Jumbo. But to her astonishment and horror, a deep, hollow voice came to her ear.

'Is that Amelia Jane? This is Mr Mumbo-Jumbo speaking. I've heard what a bad doll you are. And I'm coming to get you, Amelia.

I'm walking up the passage now – I'm BANGING at the door. Let me in!'

Amelia listened in fright. There really *was* somebody speaking through the telephone this time – somebody who said he was *Mr Mumbo-Jumbo*!

Then she heard the footsteps stamping up the passage outside, where the clown had hidden himself. She heard the loud banging at the door, and the shouts of 'Let me in!'

'No, no – don't let him in!' she wailed, and she ran to the toy-cupboard. 'Don't open the door, toys. I'll be good. I'll never be bad again. I'll give you back your hanky, Tom, and your money, Mouse. Oh, oh, don't let Mr Mumbo-Jumbo in.'

Bang-bang-BANG! 'Let me in, I say!'

Amelia piled bricks all over herself in the

cupboard, trying to hide. Tom went to
the door of the nursery and spoke sternly
through it.

'Go away, Mr Mumbo-Jumbo. We will let
you know if Amelia Jane is naughty again,
and you can come and get her then.'

And to Amelia's great relief she heard

footsteps stamping away from the door, and the banging stopped.

'Well, we've saved you from your friend, Mr Mumbo-Jumbo,' said Tom, looking into the cupboard. 'Are you going to behave yourself now, or not?'

'Oh, yes, yes,' sobbed Amelia Jane. 'Oh, that awful toy telephone. I'll never use it again.'

She didn't, of course. And, strange to say, neither did Mr Mumbo-Jumbo!

Now then, Amelia Jane!

Amelia Jane, the big naughty doll in the nursery, was doing a bit of sewing. She sat in the corner, her head bent over her work, sewing away.

'Aha! So you've decided to sew on that shoe button at last!' said the clockwork clown, coming up. 'Quite time, too – your shoe's fallen off heaps of times!'

'You be quiet,' said Amelia Jane.

'And while you're about it, why not mend that hole in your dress?' said a wooden skittle, hopping up. 'Or do you *like* holes in your dress, Amelia Jane?'

'You be quiet, too,' said Amelia, and

jabbed at him with her needle. He hopped
away with a chuckle.

He was soon back again. 'And what about
your right stocking?' he said. 'It's got a great

big hole in the heel. And what about . . . ?'

Amelia Jane jabbed at him again so hard that the thimble flew off her finger. It rolled away over the floor into a corner.

'Bother you, skittle!' said Amelia Jane, in a temper. 'Now you go and pick up that thimble and bring it back to me! Why do you tease me like this? I don't like you.'

'Shan't pick up your thimble!' said the skittle, enjoying himself. 'Silly old Amelia Jane!'

'Stop yelling at one another, and you go and pick up the thimble, skittle,' said the teddy bear, crossly. 'Can't you see I'm trying to read?'

The skittle didn't dare to disobey the big fat bear. He had once been rude to the bear and the bear had sat on him for a whole day, and the skittle hadn't liked that at all. The bear was so heavy.

So he picked up the thimble – but he didn't give it back to Amelia Jane. No – he put it on his head for a hat! Then he walked up and down in a very silly way, saying, 'Look at my new hat! Oh, *do* look at my new hat!'

Everybody looked, of course, and all the toys laughed at the skittle because he really did look funny in a thimble-hat.

He took it off and bowed to them, and then put it back again.

'*Will* you give me my thimble?' cried Amelia Jane, in a rage. 'Give it to me AT ONCE!'

'Say "please", Amelia,' said the bear. 'You sound very rude.'

'I *shan't* say "please"!' cried Amelia. 'And

don't you interfere. Skittle, if you don't give me back my thimble at once I'll chase you and knock you over!'

'Can't catch *me*! Can't catch *me*!' said the skittle, who was really being very funny and very annoying. He ran here and there, and he kept taking his thimble-hat on and off to

Amelia in a very ridiculous way.

Well, Amelia Jane wasn't going to let a skittle be cheeky to her, so up she got. She raced after the skittle, and he rushed away. But Amelia Jane caught him – and do you know what she did? Instead of taking the thimble off his head, she pushed it so hard that it went right over the poor skittle's nose, and he couldn't see a thing.

'Oh! Oh, it's so tight now I can't get it off!' yelled the skittle, trying to force the thimble off his head.

Amelia Jane laughed.

'That'll teach you to wear my thimble for a hat and be so rude to me,' she said.

'Help, help!' shouted the skittle. 'It's hurting me! Oooooooooh! Ow! OOOOOOOOOOH!'

'It really *is* hurting him,' said the bear,

getting up. 'Dear, dear – I shall never finish my book today. Stand still, you silly skittle. I'll take the thimble off.'

Well, he tugged and he pulled, and he pulled and he tugged – but he couldn't get that thimble off!

Then Tom the toy soldier came up and had a try – but he couldn't get the thimble off either.

Amelia Jane tried – but it wasn't a bit of good; that thimble was jammed so hard on the skittle's head that it really could *not* be moved!

'You'll have to wear the thimble always,' said the bear at last.

The skittle lay down and yelled. 'I can't! I don't want to! Take it off, take it off! It's tight, I tell you!'

'We'll simply *have* to do something,' said Tom. 'Else the skittle will go on yelling for ever, and I don't think I could bear that.'

'Of *course* something must be done,' said the other skittles, who had popped up, looking very worried. 'Amelia Jane is very naughty.'

'That's nothing new,' said the bear.

'Dear me, do stop yelling, skittle. You'll wake up the household!'

Then the bear thought of something. 'Oh, I've got an idea,' he said. 'What about going out to ask the little pixie who lives in the pansy bed if he knows of a spell to help us. A Get-Loose Spell, perhaps.'

'A good idea,' said Tom. 'Amelia Jane, go and find the pixie and ask him.'

'What! In the middle of a dark night!' said Amelia Jane. 'No, thank you. And anyway, I don't like that pixie!'

'Amelia Jane, if you don't go and ask him, we shall take your best ribbon and hide it,' said the bear.

'Oh, no, don't do that!' said Amelia. 'It's my party ribbon. All right, you horrid things – I'll go. But I know a very good way of getting the thimble off the skittle.'

'How?' asked the toys.

'Chop off his head!' said Amelia Jane. 'He has so few brains that he'd never even notice his head was gone!'

'We *will* take away your best ribbon now,' said the bear, as the skittle gave a loud yell of fright.

'No, no – I didn't mean it!' said Amelia Jane. 'I'll go this very minute to find the pixie.'

Well, off she went, climbing out of the window and down to the pansy bed.

The little pixie was there, wide awake.

'Pixie,' began Amelia, 'I want your help.'

'What will you give me for it?' asked the pixie, at once. He didn't like Amelia.

'Nothing,' said Amelia. 'Oh – let go of my foot, you horrid little pixie!'

'I'm taking your shoe for payment,' said the pixie. 'And the other one too. They will fit me nicely. Now, it's no good yelling. I've got them. I've no doubt you've been just as naughty as usual, so it serves you right.

Now – what do you want my help for?'

Amelia Jane told him sulkily. 'The skittle is wearing my thimble jammed down hard on his head. How can we get it off?'

'Make the thimble bigger, of course,' said the pixie. 'Then his head will be too small for it and it will slip off.'

'But how can we make the thimble bigger?' asked Amelia Jane.

'Easy,' said the pixie. 'If you heat anything made of metal it becomes just a tiny bit larger – so heat the thimble, Amelia – and it will slip off the skittle's head.'

'But how can we heat it?' said Amelia, not really believing the pixie.

'Stand him on his head in hot water,' said the pixie. 'You could have thought of that yourself. Now go away. I want to try on your shoes.'

Amelia went back to the nursery. 'The pixie says that if we stand the skittle on his head in hot water, the thimble will get a bit larger and slip off,' said Amelia.

'I don't believe a word of it,' said the bear.

'Well, that's what he *said*,' said Amelia. 'He didn't tell me anything else. And I had to give him my shoes for that advice.'

'Hm,' said Tom. 'Well, poor old skittle – we'd better try it, anyway. Bear, put a little hot water into the basin, will you? Don't put the plug in in case it gets too deep – just let the water run in and out, and we'll pop the skittle in on his head, and heat the thimble in the water.'

Well, the skittle howled and yelled and kicked up a great fuss, but the bear and the

toy soldier were very firm with him. They
turned him upside down and held him in the
hot water, so that the heat warmed up the
thimble on his head.

And will you believe it? – the thimble
slipped off, just as the pixie had said it would.
But alas – it rolled round the basin, and
disappeared down the plughole! It was gone!

'Oh – my thimble, my thimble!' yelled Amelia Jane. But it was gone for good. Nobody ever saw it again.

'Serves you right, Amelia,' said the bear, turning the poor skittle the right way up again. 'Well, who would have thought the pixie knew a spell like that? Did *you* know that heat made things just a bit bigger, clockwork clown?'

'I never did,' said the clown.

But the funny thing is that it's *true*! So if ever a thimble gets stuck on one of your skittles you'll know what to do – stand him on his head in hot water and it will slip off!

And now Amelia Jane can't *bear* doing her mending, because she hasn't got a thimble and she pricks her finger all the time. Still, as the toys tell her – it's her own fault!

Amelia Jane Gets Into Trouble

Amelia Jane, as you all know, is a very clever and very naughty doll. The toys could never keep pace with her tricks – but one day she got herself into trouble.

It happened like this. Billy came into the nursery and looked round for his soldier doll. 'Tom, where are you?' he said. 'I'm going to take you to tea with me this afternoon and I'm going in *my* soldier things, too! We're going to play with Betty and Dick, and they're going to dress up as soldiers as well. So, with you, we'll be four soldiers! We'll have fun!'

He began looking for Tom, the soldier. But
before he could find him his mother called
out. 'Billy! Come here a minute. I want you.'

Billy ran out. Amelia Jane sat up, her eyes
gleaming. 'Tom, don't you go! They'll do
awful things to you!'

'Oh dear!' said Tom, in alarm. Although

he was a soldier doll, he wasn't at all brave really. 'Oh dear! I don't want to go. I really don't!'

'Well, I'll go instead,' said Amelia Jane, in a kind voice. 'I'll do you a good turn and put on your clothes and go instead of you. Would you like that?'

'Oh, yes!' said Tom. He stripped off his soldier clothes, and Amelia Jane dressed herself up in them. My word, she did look different. You should have seen her! She pranced about looking very smart in Tom's trousers and jacket. 'I'm grand! I'm brave!'

She began to rush at the toys, pretending to capture them. They didn't like it at all.

'Now stop that, Amelia Jane!' said the sailor doll. 'And take off those clothes. You know perfectly well that nobody will harm

Tom if he goes out to tea – you've only said that because you want to dress up and prance about pretending to be a soldier. Take those clothes off.'

But all that Amelia Jane did was to rush at the toy clown and the sailor doll, and pretend to capture them. They were very cross indeed – but Amelia was bigger than they were, and it was difficult to stop her.

In rushed Billy. He caught hold of Amelia Jane, thinking she was Tom, his soldier doll. Out of the door he went at top speed, calling out, 'I'm ready, Mother! I'm just coming!'

Amelia Jane planned to have a wonderful time. She would go stalking Betty and Dick with Billy. She would take them prisoner. My goodness, Amelia Jane was going to have the time of her life!

But it didn't turn out quite like that. Billy, Betty and Dick got the gardener to hide Amelia Jane somewhere, so that they could stalk her and pounce on her and take her prisoner!

So Amelia was put into the middle of a bush by the gardener, and left there. The children began to hunt for her, going along in single file, leaping high in the air, and filling the garden with loud cries.

Amelia Jane shivered in the bush. How
she hoped they wouldn't find her. She didn't
mind stalking the others and pouncing on
them – but she didn't want to be pounced
on and taken prisoner herself!

Well, the children soon found her. They
surrounded the bush, and Betty yelled out
loudly: 'The enemy is hiding here! I see him!
Come on, soldiers, come on!'

And they all pounced! Amelia Jane was
pulled roughly from the bush and thrown
to the ground.

'You're our prisoner!' yelled the three,
and ran round her. They didn't even touch
Amelia, but she thought they were going to
every time they came.

'Let's tie him to a tree,' said Billy. So they

took Amelia and tied her to a little tree.

'Funny sort of doll, this,' said Dick, looking closely at her. 'He's got a face more like a girl-doll than a boy-doll.'

'Now he's tied up. He can't get away. He's our prisoner,' said Betty.

But fortunately for Amelia Jane, the tea-bell rang loudly, and the three soldiers raced up to the house in glee.

Amelia Jane began to sob. She struggled with the knots that tied her, but they were tight and she couldn't undo even one of them. She was very frightened. How she wished she hadn't been silly enough to make Tom give her his clothes!

'I'm always doing silly things!' wept Amelia. 'I wish I didn't. Oh, what shall I do?'

She waited for the children to come back. She waited and she waited. But they didn't come. Betty's mother had said she thought it was going to rain, so they could either play a *quiet* game of soldiers indoors, or a noisy game of snap, whichever they liked.

They chose snap, and forgot all about Amelia Jane, tied to the tree in the garden. In fact Billy forgot about her completely, and even went home without her! So there

she was when darkness came, still tied up tightly, jumping in fright every time an owl came by and hooted.

The toys were surprised when Billy came home without Amelia Jane. He didn't say anything about leaving her behind until just before he went to bed. He was sitting in his pyjamas eating his supper in the nursery with his sister, when he suddenly gave a cry.

'What's the matter?' said his mother.

'It's Tom. I've forgotten to bring him home,' said Billy. 'We tied him up to a tree and then we went in to tea and I forgot all about him. He's still there, poor thing. And it's dark and rainy. Mother, I must go and get him.'

'No, you mustn't,' said his mother, firmly. 'You are certainly not going to run down the dark rainy street in your pyjamas. You can get Tom tomorrow. If he's under a tree he won't get very wet.'

'But he'll be frightened,' said Billy. 'He won't like it.'

'Well, that's your fault,' said his mother. 'When we forget things we often make others suffer as well as ourselves. You should have remembered to bring Tom home.'

Now, of course, the toys couldn't help hearing all this, because they were sitting round the nursery watching the children eat their supper. They were full of horror.

What! Amelia Jane tied up to a tree, left alone in the darkness and the rain! Naughty as she was, and cross as they felt with her, they were very sorry. When the children had gone to bed they got together in a corner and talked about it.

'I'll go and rescue her,' said Tom, bravely. 'I know the way. I've been to that house before.'

'But you haven't got any clothes on,' said the sailor doll. 'You'll get soaked. And it's frightening to go out in the dark at night. You might meet a fierce dog or a yowling cat who would pounce on you. Anyway, you're not very brave.'

'Oh, I know that,' said Tom, sadly. 'It's a pity to have to be a soldier doll and not feel brave. That's really why I'm going. I'm not brave, in fact I'm very frightened, but I feel I *ought* to be brave, so I'm going to rescue Amelia.'

'Well, that's very nice of you, after she tricked you into taking off your clothes and letting her go out to tea instead of you,' said the toy clown, patting Tom on the back.

'All right, you go then, if you know the way.
What about clothes? There's a little cape and
hat in the doll's wardrobe. You could borrow
those.'

So Tom put them on and he looked rather
odd, not at all like a soldier doll! Then he
slipped out of the window, climbed down the
tree outside and set off in the darkness to
Betty's house.

The rain hit him on the nose, and ran down his cloak in little rivers. It went down his neck too, because his hat didn't fit very well. At last he came to the garden of Betty's house and slipped through a hole in the fence.

Amelia Jane was still tied to the tree. An owl had hooted in her ear. A spider had walked over her face. A hedgehog had walked so near that his spines pricked her legs. She was lonely and scared.

She heard a noise. What was that? Oh, what was that? It sounded like someone coming nearer and nearer, creeping through the bushes! Amelia began to tremble and shake.

'Who is it? Go away! Leave me alone! Oh, don't come near me, I'm scared, I'm frightened! Don't frighten me any more.

Go away, whoever it is!'

But the footsteps came nearer and nearer, and then a head poked round a bush. Amelia Jane gave a scream.

'Go away! I'm frightened of you!'

Well it was Tom, of course, come to rescue her! 'It's all right,' he said. 'It's only me, Tom. I'll undo your knots, Amelia Jane.'

Amelia could have hugged him! Dear, dear Tom! Oh, how could she have tricked him like that! She would always, always love him now.

He undid the knots. She stretched herself stiffly and then sneezed. 'Let's hurry home,' said Tom. 'You've caught a cold. I'll lead the way.'

Well, it wasn't long before they were both back in the nursery again, leaving little wet marks all over the floor. As soon as they got there Amelia Jane flung herself on Tom and hugged him so hard that he squealed.

'Good, kind, *brave* Tom! Oh, what courage you've got! Oh, how plucky you are! Toys, Tom is quite the bravest toy in the nursery!'

Tom could hardly believe his ears when all the toys crowded round and thumped him on the back, and said the same as Amelia! 'But I'm not brave!' he kept saying. 'I never have been! I was frightened all the time. Brave people aren't frightened.'

'The bravest people of all are those who are frightened and yet go on being brave,' said the sailor doll, helping him off with his wet cloak. 'Amelia Jane has no right to wear a soldier's clothes – she's a little coward! As soon as they are dry, you must wear them again, because you really and truly are a brave soldier!'

The toys dried Tom's clothes, as soon as Amelia Jane had taken them off. Amelia dressed humbly in her own clothes. She felt ashamed of herself. She sneezed loudly.

'I'm getting a dreadful cold,' she said, very sorry for herself.

'It serves you right,' said the sailor doll. 'Don't sneeze all over us, please. We're giving a party for Tom soon, and you'd better not come in case you give everyone your cold.'

So now Amelia Jane is sitting by herself in a corner sneezing into her hanky, watching the most wonderful party going on, given for Tom, the soldier doll. Nobody feels at all sorry for her. I don't know if you do?

Billy's going to be very surprised tomorrow to find that Tom is sitting in the nursery instead of tied up to the tree! He's going to puzzle about that for days.

Amelia Jane Has a Good Idea

The new teddy bear was very small indeed.
The toys stared at him when he first came
into the playroom, wondering what he was.

'Good gracious! I believe you're a teddy
bear!' said Amelia Jane, the big, naughty doll.
'I thought you were a peculiar-shaped
mouse.'

'Well, I'm not,' said the small bear, sharply,
and pressed himself in the middle. 'Grrrrrr!
Hear me growl? Well, no mouse can growl.
It can only squeak.'

'Yes. You're a bear all right,' said Tom,
coming up. 'I hear you've come to live with
us. Well, I'll show you your place in the

toy-cupboard – right at the back there, look.'

'I don't like being at the back, it's too dark,' said the little bear. 'I'll be at the front here, by this big brick-box.'

'Oh, no you won't. That's *my* place when I want to sit in the toy-cupboard,' said Amelia Jane. 'And let me tell you this, small bear – if you live with us you'll have to take on lots of little bits of work. We all do. You'll have to wind up the clockwork clown when he runs down, you'll have to clean the dolls'-house windows, and you'll have to help the engine-driver polish his big red train.'

'Dear me, I don't think I want to do any of those things,' said the bear. 'I'm lazy. I don't like working.'

'Well, you'll just have to,' said Amelia Jane. 'Otherwise you won't get any of the biscuit

crumbs that the children drop on the floor,
you won't get any of the sweets in the toy
sweet-shop – and we're allowed some every
week – and you won't come to any parties.
So there.'

'Pooh!' said the bear and stalked off to pick
up some beads out of the bead-box and

thread himself a necklace.

'He's vain as well as lazy,' said Tom in disgust. 'Hey, bear – what's your name? Or are you too lazy to have one?'

'My name is Sidney Gordon Eustace,' said the bear, haughtily. 'And please remember that I don't like being called Sid.'

'Sid!' yelled all the toys at once, and the bear looked furious. He turned his head away, and went on threading the beads.

'Sidney Gordon Eustace!' said the clown, with a laugh. 'I guess he gave himself those names. No sensible child would ever call a teddy bear that. Huh!'

The bear was not much use in the playroom. He just would *not* do any of the jobs there at all. He went surprisingly deaf when anyone called to him to come and clean or polish or sweep. He would pretend to be asleep, or just walk about humming a little tune as if nobody was calling his name at all. It was most annoying.

'Sidney! Come and shake the mats for the dolls'-house dolls!' Tom called. No answer from Sidney at all.

'SIDNEY! Come here! You're not as deaf as all that!'

The bear never even turned his head.

'Hey, Sidney Gordon Eustace – come and do your jobs!' yelled Tom. 'SID, SID, SID!'

No answer. 'All right!' shouted Tom, angrily. 'You shan't have that nice big crumb of chocolate biscuit we found under the table this morning.'

It was always the same whenever there was a job to be done. 'Sidney, come here!' But Sidney never came. He never did one single thing for any of the toys.

'What are we going to do about him?' said the big teddy bear. 'Amelia Jane – can't you think of a good idea?'

'Oh, yes,' said Amelia at once. 'I know what we'll do. We'll get Sidney-the-mouse to come and do the things that Sidney-the-bear should do – and he shall have all the crumbs and titbits that the bear should have. He won't like that – a little house-mouse getting all his treats!'

'Dear me – is the house-mouse's name Sidney, too?' said Tom in surprise. 'I never knew that before. When we want him we usually go to his hole and shout, "Mouse" and he comes.'

'Well, I'll go and shout "Sidney",' said
Amelia Jane, 'and you'll see – he'll come!' So
she went to the little hole at the bottom of the
wall near the bookcase and shouted down it.

'Sidney! Sid-Sid-Sidney! We want you!'

The little bear, of course, didn't turn round
– *he* wasn't going to come when his name
was called. But someone very small came
scampering up the passage to the hole-
entrance. It was the tiny brown house-mouse,
with bright black eyes and twitching whiskers.

'Ah, Sidney,' said Amelia Jane. 'Will you
just come and shake the mats in the dolls'
house, please? They are very dusty. We'll
give you a big chocolate biscuit crumb and
a drink of lemonade out of the little teapot if
you will.'

'Can I drink out of the spout?' said the tiny mouse, pleased. 'I like drinking out of the spout.'

'Yes, of course,' said Amelia Jane.

The little mouse set about shaking the mats vigorously, and the job was soon done.

'Isn't Sidney wonderful?' said Amelia in a loud voice to the others. 'Sidney-the-mouse, I mean, of course, not silly Sidney-the-bear. He wouldn't have the strength to shake mats like that, poor thing. Sidney, here's the chocolate biscuit crumb and there's the teapot full of lemonade.'

Sidney the bear didn't like this at all. Fancy making a fuss of a silly little mouse, and giving him treats like that. He would very much have liked the crumb and the lemonade himself. He pressed himself in the middle and growled furiously when the mouse had gone.

'Don't have that mouse here again,' he said. 'I don't like hearing somebody else being called Sidney. Anyway, I don't believe his name *is* Sidney. It's not a name for a mouse.'

'Well, for all you know, his name might be Sidney Gordon Eustace just like yours,' said Amelia Jane at once.

'Pooh! Whoever heard of a mouse having a grand name like that?' said the bear.

'Well, next time you won't do a job, we'll call all three names down the hole,' said Amelia, 'and see if the little mouse will answer to them!'

Next night there was going to be a party. Everyone had to help to get ready for it. Amelia Jane called to the little bear.

'Sidney! Come and set the tables for the party. Sidney, do you hear me?'

Sidney did, but he pretended not to, of course. Set party tables! Not he! So he went deaf again, and didn't even turn his head.

'Sidney Gordon Eustace, do as you're told or you won't come to the party,' bawled the big teddy bear in a fine old rage.

The little bear didn't answer. Amelia Jane gave a sudden grin.

'Never mind,' she said. 'We'll get Sidney Gordon Eustace, the little mouse, to come and set the tables. He does them beautifully and never breaks a thing. He can come to the party afterwards then. I'll call him.'

The little bear turned his head. 'He won't answer to *that* name, you know he won't!' he said, scornfully. 'Call away! No mouse ever had a name as grand as mine.'

Amelia Jane went to the mouse-hole and called down it.

'Sidney Gordon Eustace, are you there?' she called. 'If you are at home, come up and help us. Sidney Gordon Eustace, are you there?'

And at once there came the pattering of tiny feet, and with a loud squeak the little mouse peeped out of his hole, his whiskers quivering.

'Ah – you are at home,' said Amelia. 'Well, dear little Sidney, will you set the tables for us? We're going to have a party.'

The mouse was delighted. He was soon

at work, and in a short while the four tables
were set with tiny table-cloths and china.
Then he went to help the dolls'-house dolls to
cut sandwiches. The bear watched all this out
of the corner of his eye. He was quite amazed
that the mouse had come when he was called
Sidney Gordon Eustace – goodness, fancy a

little mouse owning a name like that!

He was very cross when he saw that the mouse was going to the party. Amelia Jane found him a red ribbon to tie round his neck and one for his long tail. He was given a place at the biggest table, and everyone made a fuss of him.

'Good little Sidney! You do work well! Whatever should we do without you? What will you have to eat?'

The mouse ate a lot. *Much* too much, the little bear thought. He didn't go to the party. He hadn't been asked and he didn't quite like to go because there was no chair for him and no plate. But, oh, all those nice things to eat! *Why* hadn't he been sensible and gone to set the tables?

'Goodnight, Sidney Gordon Eustace,' said

Amelia to the delighted mouse. 'We've loved having you.'

Now, after this kind of thing had happened three or four times the bear got tired of it.

He hated hearing people yell for 'Sidney, Sidney!' down the mouse-hole, or to hear the mouse addressed as Sidney Gordon Eustace. It was really too bad. Also, the mouse was getting all the titbits and the treats. The bear didn't like that either.

So the next time that there was a job to be done the bear decided to do it. He suddenly heard Tom say 'Hallo! The big red engine is very smeary. It wants a polish again. I'll go and call Sidney.'

Tom went to the mouse-hole and began to call down it. 'Sidney, Sidney, Sidney!'

But before the mouse could answer,

Sidney the bear rushed up to Tom. 'Yes! Did you call me? What do you want me to do?'

'Dear me – you're not as deaf as usual!' said Tom, surprised. 'Well, go and polish the red engine, then. You can have a sweet out of the toy sweet shop if you do it properly.'

Sidney did do it properly. Tom came and looked at the engine and so did Amelia Jane. 'Very nice,' said Amelia. 'Give him a big sweet, Tom.'

The bear was pleased. Aha! He had done the mouse out of a job. The toys had been pleased with him, and the sweet was delicious.

And after that, dear me, you should have seen Sidney the bear rush up whenever his name was called. 'Yes, yes – here I am. What do you want me to do?'

Very soon the little mouse was not called up from the hole any more, and Sidney the bear worked hard and was friendly and sensible. The toys began to like him, and Sidney liked them too.

But one thing puzzled Tom and the big

teddy bear, and they asked Amelia Jane about it.

'Amelia Jane – HOW did you know that the mouse's name was Sidney Gordon Eustace?'

'It isn't,' said Amelia with a grin.

'But it must be,' said Tom. 'He always came when you called him by it.'

'I know – but he'd come if you called *any* name down his hole,' said Amelia. 'Go and call what name you like – he'll come! It's the calling he answers, not the name! He doesn't even know what names are!'

'Good gracious!' said Tom and the bear, and they went to the mouse-hole.

'William!' called Tom, and up came the mouse. He was given a crumb and went down again.

'Polly-Wolly-Doodle!' shouted the big bear, and up came the mouse for another crumb.

'Boot-polish!' shouted Tom, and up came the mouse.

'Tomato soup!' cried the big bear. And it didn't matter what name was yelled down the hole, the mouse always came up. He came because he heard a loud shout, that was all. Amelia Jane went off into fits of laughter when the mouse came up at different calls. 'Penny stamp! Cough-drop! Sid-Sid-Sid!

Dickory-Dock! Rub-a-dub-dub!'

The mouse's nose appeared at the hole each time. How the toys laughed – all except Sidney the bear!

He didn't laugh. He felt very silly indeed. Oh, dear – what a trick Amelia Jane had played on him! But suddenly he began to laugh, too. 'It's funny,' he cried. 'It's funny!'

It certainly was. Amelia *would* think of a good idea like that, wouldn't she?

Amelia Jane is Very Busy

One day Amelia Jane sat very still in her little chair, and watched somebody knitting in the playroom. It was little Miss Jones, who came to help with the children's clothes. She was knitting a jersey for the biggest boy.

'Click–click–clickety–click!' Her knitting needles flashed in and out all day long, and Amelia Jane watched and watched.

When little Miss Jones had finished all the knitting and had put the balls of left–over wool neatly in the work-basket with the long needles, she left the playroom to go home.

As soon as she had gone Amelia Jane ran to the work-basket. She took up two needles and a ball of wool and went to sit on the rug by herself, leaning against the table-leg.

'I can knit,' she told the toys. 'I know how to. I watched Miss Jones all day long. You go like this – and like that – and see, the knitting comes!'

The toys watched her. They thought Amelia Jane was very clever. Click-click-clickity-click – why, her needles went as fast as Miss Jones' needles!

'What are you making?' asked the sailor doll.

'Nothing. I'm just knitting,' said Amelia.

'But you must be knitting *something*,' said the clockwork mouse. 'You can't just *knit*.'

'It's a waste of wool not to make something when you knit,' said the teddy bear. 'Can't you make me a jersey?'

'No. It would take me ages to knit a jersey to go over your fat little tummy,' said Amelia Jane.

'Don't be rude,' said the bear, offended. 'If *you* kept a growl in your tummy, you'd be fat, too. Grrr!'

'Couldn't you knit me a bonnet?' said the baby doll. 'I could do with a new one.'

'No, I couldn't. You've got three already,' said Amelia Jane. 'For goodness' sake go away and let me *knit*! I tell you, I'm not making anything at all, I'm just knitting.'

The baby doll sat down by her and took off her hair-ribbon to smooth it out. She was very particular about her ribbons. She put it down beside her, and began to comb out her hair with a little comb.

'Go away,' said Amelia. 'I don't like people who comb hair all over me.'

'Well, you can just put up with it,' said the baby doll, crossly. 'I can sit where I like.'

Amelia Jane didn't say anything – but when the baby doll looked for her hair-ribbon it had gone!

'You've taken it!' she said to Amelia. 'You mean thing. Give it back.'

'She can't. She's knitted it with the wool!' said Tom, pointing. And sure enough that bad Amelia Jane had taken the ribbon and knitted it – and there was the ribbon, right in the very middle of the knitting.

'I can't take it out,' said Amelia. 'It would spoil my beautiful knitting. You'll have to do without your ribbon now. It's your own fault.'

The baby doll went off, crying. 'Cry-baby!' said Amelia Jane, and went on knitting.

'Your knitting is nothing but a long, long scarf, very narrow,' said the bear. 'It's silly knitting. Nobody would wear a scarf like that.'

'Nobody's going to,' said Amelia Jane. 'I wish you would stop bothering me. Can't I knit if I want to?'

'The click-click noise makes me cross,' said the sailor doll.

'It doesn't take much to make you cross,' said Amelia. 'Clockwork mouse, what do *you* want? Don't you dare to nibble my wool!'

'I just want to watch you knit,' said the mouse, and he sat down close by. And will you believe it, that rascally Amelia Jane knitted his long tail into her knitting!

The little mouse suddenly found himself pulled towards Amelia's knitting, and saw his tail there!

Goodness, what a to-do there was! The bear was very angry. 'You can't do things like this, Amelia!' he said.

'I can,' she said. 'And I have. The mouse can't have his tail back. It belongs to my knitting now.'

But the sailor doll made her undo the tail because the clockwork mouse was so upset.

'He can't hang on to your knitting by his tail,' he told Amelia Jane.

'You're very unkind and very silly. Just *look* at the enormous length of knitting you have done – all for nothing, too!'

The next thing he knew was that Amelia had pulled out his bootlaces and had knitted

those, too! She would not give them back, either, and the sailor doll stamped round the nursery in a rage, his boots slipping off his feet every minute!

'She'll have to fall asleep sometime soon,' whispered the teddy bear to the toy soldier. 'Then we'll pay her out for all this!'

So they waited till her needles worked more and more slowly – clickity-click, clickity-click – click – click – click – click – and then they stopped. Amelia Jane was fast asleep!

The toys crept up to her. They took up the long, long strip of knitting. They wound it all round Amelia Jane and the table-leg she was leaning against – round and round and round and round!

'Now she's all tied up in her own knitting!' said Tom, pleased. 'And the more she knits, the more tied up she will get.'

Amelia Jane woke up merry and bright. She picked up her knitting needles and started off again – clickity-click, clickity-click!

But soon she found that she was bound tightly to the table-leg, and the more she pulled at her knitting, the tighter it became. She tried to stand up – but she couldn't.

'Oh! Oh! I've knitted myself to the table-leg!' she cried. 'Toys, help me!'

'Certainly *not*,' said the clockwork clown with a squeal of delight. 'Go on knitting. You'll soon be right in the middle of it and we shan't see you again! Knit hard, Amelia, knit hard!'

Amelia Jane didn't. She stopped. She tugged at the knitting to try to free herself but she couldn't. And dear me, how scared she got when she saw how the knitting was wound round and round and round herself and the table-leg!

'Undo me!' she begged the baby doll.

'I will if you knit me a new bonnet,' said the doll.

'Undo me!' Amelia Jane begged the bear.

'I will if you knit me a jersey and don't say anything about my fat little tummy,' said the bear.

'And you can knit me a red waistcoat,' said Tom.

'And me a new vest,' said the sailor doll.

'All right,' said Amelia. 'You're mean, all of you. But I'll knit what you want – and I hope nothing fits, so there!'

Well, they undid Amelia Jane from the table-leg, and then they helped her to pull undone all the long, long piece of knitting.

Out came the sailor's bootlaces and the baby doll's ribbon!

And then she had to set to work to keep her promises. She has made the bear a tight little red jersey.

'You'll never be able to get it off again, once you've got it on,' Tom told him, so the poor bear can't make up his mind whether to wear it or not.

Amelia has made the sailor a new vest, but as it reaches down to his feet he doesn't quite know what to do with it!

As for Tom's waistcoat, it's got three armholes instead of two! 'Use one for a leg!' said Amelia with a giggle. But how can he do that?

And now Amelia is knitting the bonnet for the baby doll, but as it is already big enough to go all round the teddy bear's middle, I expect she will have to use it for a shawl!

Can't you be sensible, Amelia Jane – just for once? Tie her up to the table-leg again, toys! She's just too bad for words.

Oh, Bother, Amelia Jane!

'What are you doing, Amelia Jane?' asked the sailor doll. 'What do you want that water for?'

'I'm going to paint,' said Amelia. 'See, I've found a paintbox in the toy-cupboard. I know how to paint because I've watched the children.'

'How do you paint?' asked the sailor doll.

Amelia Jane dipped her paintbrush into the water and then rubbed it on one of the little squares of colour in the paintbox.

'I paint like this!' she said with a giggle and splashed a big stripe of green all across the sailor doll's face!

He was very angry. He went off to tell the
other toys. 'She's in one of her silly moods
again,' he said to Tom. 'We'd better look
out!'

Amelia Jane painted hard all the morning.
At first she painted pictures on a piece of
paper. Then she looked round for something
better to do with her paints.

'The dolls' house! I'll paint monkeys
climbing up the wall,' she said. 'The little
dolls have gone out for a walk – they'll
be surprised when they come back!'

So she painted little brown monkeys all the
way up the front walls of the pretty little dolls'
house – they did look peculiar!

The dolls'-house dolls screamed when they

came back. 'Look! What's that on the walls? Monkeys! Are they real? Oh, what's happened to our dear little house?'

'You be careful in case there are monkeys inside it too!' said Amelia Jane, and not one of the tiny dolls dared to go in at their front door!

Then she saw the little wooden train standing by itself in a corner of the room. The engine-driver had gone to talk to the teddy bear, so he wasn't there. Amelia Jane took her pot of water and paintbox – and do you know what she did? She painted rows of silly faces all round the engine and its trucks!

'Look! What's happened? Where did these dreadful faces come from?' cried the engine-driver when he saw them. 'My beautiful train! Everyone will laugh at me when I drive it.'

'You'd better get a cloth and rub all the
faces off,' said Tom. 'Bother Amelia Jane!
I'll help you, Engine-driver.'

So they spent a long, long time trying to
get the faces off the engine and the train.
They were very hot and tired by the end of it.

'I'd be much obliged if you would go and
give Amelia Jane a good telling-off from me,'
said the engine-driver. 'I'm too small to do it
myself.'

'With pleasure,' said Tom and he went up to Amelia Jane, and gave her a good scolding. She was very angry – and you can guess what she did! She painted his hat white when he was asleep!

It did look strange.

He was very much upset. All the toys stood round him and giggled.

'What happened?' said the teddy bear. 'Your hat's all white, Tom!'

Tom had to climb up to the little wash-basin, turn on a tap, put the plug in, and try to wash the white off his hat. He managed to get himself wet all over, and the white ran down his jacket and trousers.

So then he had to sit in front of the fire, and when his jacket dried it shrank and was so tight that he could hardly breathe.

He was very, very cross with Amelia Jane!

She painted the clockwork mouse's tail a bright red, and he thought it was a worm running after him. He raced away, squealing, 'I can't get away from that red worm; it follows me, it follows me!' The toys couldn't help laughing.

'It's only your tail. Don't be afraid of your own tail,' said the bear. 'Go and climb up to the bookshelf, where the bowl of goldfish is. Sit on the edge and dip your tail into the water. The red will run off and you will be all right again.'

'Yes, you do that,' said Amelia Jane, with a grin. *She* knew what would happen, but the others didn't! The clockwork mouse got up on to the bookcase, and went to the goldfish bowl. He sat on the edge and dipped his red tail into the water.

The goldfish were very excited. 'A worm! A lovely long red worm!' they bubbled to one another. 'Quick, catch it and eat it!'

And they swam to the little red tail and snapped at it. Goodness – the mouse almost fell backwards into the water! 'Don't! Don't! That's my tail!' he squealed.

He only just managed to get it out of the bowl before it was nibbled off. He raced down to the floor, tumbling over and over when he got there.

Amelia Jane laughed and laughed. The clockwork mouse cried bitterly. 'I wish *you* had a tail!' he said to Amelia Jane. 'I'd come and nibble it, then you'd know how it felt!'

Now the next night, a small mouse, a real one this time, came running out of a hole in the playroom wall with a little note in his mouth. It was from the toys in the next house.

'I say!' said the clockwork clown, reading the note. 'The toys next door are giving a fancy dress party! What fun! It's the night after next. Well, *I* shall go as a pirate!'

'I shall go as one of the bears in the story of The Three Bears,' said the teddy bear.

'And I shall make myself a red cloak and hood and go as Red Riding Hood,' said the tiny doll in the corner of the toy-cupboard.

'I shall go as a queen,' said Amelia Jane, grandly. 'I can easily make myself a crown, and there's a beautiful dress laid away in a box in one of the drawers over there. I can make a cloak, and I have got a very pretty necklace that came out of a cracker.'

Well, Amelia Jane worked very hard indeed at making the lovely cloak. It was royal purple and she sewed tiny silver beads all over it, from the bead box. She tried on her crown – how lovely she looked! She put on the necklace.

'Don't I look beautiful?' she said to the
other toys. 'I shall win the first prize for
the fancy dress. I know I shall!'

Tom thought she probably would. 'You
don't deserve to,' he said. 'You've been
unkind. The clockwork mouse is still upset
because the red hasn't properly come off
his tail.'

'Pooh!' said Amelia Jane. 'You wait till I get the paintbox out again. I'll do MUCH worse things than that!'

That made the toys very angry. The bear decided to take the paintbox and hide it when Amelia wasn't looking. It was quite easy to do that because she was so tired that night with her hard work sewing on the silver beads that she fell asleep!

'Look at her – fast asleep!' said Tom. 'She doesn't *deserve* to win the first prize at the party. But she will!'

'She won't,' said the bear, suddenly. 'I've got an idea, Tom. Listen – *I* can paint just as well as Amelia Jane can. And I'm going to paint her face in all kinds of stripes and dots while she's asleep! It'll be red and blue and green and yellow!'

The toys stood and giggled as the bear took the paintbrush, dipped it into the little pot of water, and began to paint Amelia's sleeping face. Goodness, he did it well! Stripes of red and green, dots of blue and yellow, crosses of black and brown.

Oh dear – what a terrifying sight Amelia Jane looked!

'But she'll see herself in the mirror, won't she?' said the clockwork mouse.

'No, because she would have to climb up on the bookcase, and stand there to see herself in the mirror on the wall,' said the bear. 'And she won't do that when she's wearing a cloak. She couldn't climb in that.'

Well, when Amelia Jane woke up, she didn't know anything about her painted face, of course. All the toys put on fancy dresses for the party – and Amelia Jane couldn't *think* why they giggled every time they looked at her. In fact the clockwork mouse laughed so much that his key fell out.

Amelia walked up and down, wearing her crown and necklace, with the beautiful silk dress going 'swish–swish–swish' all the time, and her cloak flying out behind her, gleaming with silver beads. She didn't know how funny she looked, with her painted face, all stripes and dots and crosses!

'First prize for *me*!' she said to the toys. 'Don't you think so?'

That made them giggle again, of course. Amelia Jane simply couldn't understand them. 'You're being very silly tonight,' she said. 'Well – I'm just going out into the passage to look at myself in the long mirror there. I don't want to climb up to the bookcase mirror in this long cloak.'

The toys had quite forgotten *that* mirror! They wondered whatever Amelia Jane would say when she saw herself. She walked out into the passage – and then she gave a loud scream.

'Oh! OH! My face! What's happened to it?

Oh, you wicked bad toys, you've painted it! And I haven't time to wash it off properly. Oh, you horrid mean things.'

'We've only done to you what you did to us!' said Tom, grinning. 'You can't go to the party like that – and it serves you right!'

'I shall come! I shall! You just see!' cried Amelia Jane, and she took off her crown and necklace and began to undo her cloak. 'Yes, and I'll get first prize, too! Oh, you unkind things!'

'Well, we won't wait. It's time we set off,' said the bear. 'Goodbye, Amelia Jane. We are sorry we shan't see you at the fancy dress party.'

But all the same Amelia is going! I look like a majestic peacock, with all the different colours on my face! she thought, as she threw

off her lovely dress. All right – I'll go as a
peacock! Where's that little shuttle-cock with
coloured feathers set round it? They will do
for my hair!

She pulled out the feathers and set them round her head. Then she looked for the little tent that the bear and Tom sometimes played with. It was painted brightly.

'That will do for a cloak,' said Amelia. 'Toy soldier, the bear and all the rest! Look out – I'm coming to the party after all!'

And off she went at top speed, the proudest peacock you ever saw. What a shock the toys are going to get! I can only hope that naughty Amelia Jane doesn't win the first prize after all!

Goodbye, Amelia Jane!

The toys played a trick on Amelia Jane the other day.

Amelia Jane was always playing tricks on all the toys in the nursery. There was no end to her mischief. If she didn't think of one thing, she thought of another.

There was the time when she collected worms in the garden and popped them all into Tom's shut umbrella. They wriggled about there and couldn't get out, poor things.

And then Amelia sent Tom out into the garden to fetch her hanky from the garden seat. It was raining, of course, so she gave him his umbrella.

'Better put this up,' she said, and he did. And out slithered all the worms, on top of his head and down his neck, as soon as he got out into the garden in the rain.

The worms fled into holes very thankfully, but Tom got such a fright that he ran straight into the pond and got wet through.

He was very, very angry with Amelia Jane, but she only laughed.

'You shouldn't let worms nest in your umbrella,' she said.

Another time, Amelia took the teapot out of the toy tea-set and filled it with hot water from the tap. Then she climbed up to the roof of the dolls' house and poured the hot water down the chimney.

The little dolls'-house dolls rushed out of the front door in fright, with water trickling down the stairs after them, and Amelia Jane nearly fell off the roof with laughing.

She was well scolded for that bit of mischief, but she wouldn't even say she was sorry.

The toys had a meeting about her.

'I'm tired of Amelia Jane,' said the toy soldier.

'So am I,' said the clockwork clown. 'She took my key away yesterday for about the fiftieth time.'

'Can't we get rid of her?' said the teddy bear.

'We've often tried,' said the clockwork mouse. 'But we never have.'

'I've got an idea,' said Tom, his eyes shining brightly. 'It's a small idea at the moment – but if we talk about it, it might grow into a big one and be really good.'

'What is it?' asked the clockwork clown.

'Well – you know you can slide down the stairs on a tray, don't you?' said Tom.

Everyone nodded.

'That's my idea,' said Tom. 'It's only just that. I haven't thought any more than that.'

'It seems rather silly,' said the bear. 'Did you mean to get Amelia Jane to slide down the stairs on a tray, or what?'

'I don't know,' said Tom. 'I tell you, I hadn't thought any further than I said.'

'Ooooh!' said the clown. '*Could* we make her slide down on a tray – push her very, very hard . . . ?'

'And have the front door open so that she shot right out in a hurry,' went on the bear.

'And have the garden gate open so that she'd shoot out there, too,' said the clown.

'And then down the hill she'd go, whizz-bang, faster and faster and faster,' said the clockwork mouse, excitedly.

'And splash into the stream on her tray,

and off it would go like a boat, all the way down to the sea!' finished Tom, his face beaming with excitement.

'And we'd never, never see her again, the bad, naughty doll,' said the bear.

'No, we wouldn't. We'd shout, "Goodbye, Amelia Jane!" when she flew out of the front door, and that would be that,' said Tom. 'See what my little idea has grown to – a great big one. I thought it would!'

Well, the toys talked and talked about their idea, and got very excited about it indeed. Surely they could at last get rid of that naughty Amelia Jane!

Amelia didn't know anything about all this, of course. She was out in the garden collecting a few more worms to play another trick. Tom had time to get out the big tin tray from its corner and rub soap underneath it to make it more slippery.

'We'll play our trick when everyone is out tomorrow,' he decided. 'If I stand on a chair in the hall I can open the front door all right. Now, don't say a word about our plan, any of you!'

The next afternoon the house was very quiet because everyone had gone out. Tom took the tin tray and banged hard on it. 'Boom, diddy-boom!'

'Stop that noise,' said Amelia Jane, crossly. 'I want to have a snooze.'

'All right. Have one,' said Tom. 'We are all going to the top of the stairs to play at sliding down on this tea-tray. We'll have a lovely time – and we don't want *you*, Amelia Jane!'

Well, that was quite enough to make Amelia want to come, of course! 'I'm coming, too,' she said. 'And I guess I'll go faster down the stairs than any of you!'

Off they all went to the top of the stairs. Tom ran down, got a chair, stood on it, and opened the front door. He ran back and had his turn at sliding down. The tray went down to the bottom, bumpity-bumpity-bump, slid a little way down the hall and stopped. Aha! If they all pushed hard when Amelia Jane had her turn, it would most certainly fly out of the door, down the path, out of the gate and away down the hill to the stream at the bottom!

'I want my turn, I want mine!' shouted Amelia, and she got on to the tray. She held tight – and the toy soldier, the bear, the clockwork clown, the mouse and another doll all pushed as hard as ever they could.

Whoooooosh! You should have seen that tray fly down the stairs at top speed! Amelia's breath was quite taken away. Her hair and her dress flew out behind her, and she stared in fright. This was a much faster journey than she had imagined!

Down to the bottom of the stairs – along the hall at top speed – out of the open door – down the slippery front path – out of the open gate – and whoooooosh – down the steep hill that led to the stream!

'Goodbye, Amelia Jane!' shouted the toys. 'Goodbye, goodbye!'

'She's gone,' said the bear, after a pause. 'Really gone. She'll never tease us again.'

'Never,' said Tom, pleased. 'She's played her last trick on us.'

'She deserved to be shot off like that,'

said the clown. 'Now let's play at sliding trays downstairs all by ourselves.'

They played for quite a long time. Then they went back to the nursery to have a drink of water.

'I just hope Amelia Jane didn't tip off the tray going down the hill, and hurt herself,' said the bear, suddenly.

'And I just hope she didn't fall into the stream and get drowned,' said the clown.

'It seems a bit funny without her,' said the mouse. 'Er – you don't suppose we were dreadfully unkind, do you?'

'Not a bit,' said Tom. 'She deserved to be sent off like that.'

'But you wouldn't want her to hurt herself, would you?' said the bear, solemnly. 'You know – I keep on and on thinking what would happen if she tipped off the tray going downhill – suppose she fell under a bus – or . . .'

The clockwork mouse gave a squeal of fright. 'Don't say things like that. They frighten me. You make me feel as if I want Amelia Jane back.'

'Perhaps she wasn't as bad as she seemed,' said the bear. 'You know – I don't feel very nice about playing that trick on her now. I feel sort of uncomfortable.'

'Pooh!' said Tom, but he didn't say any more.

Well, what *had* happened to Amelia Jane? She had slid out into the front garden and out of the gate, and down the hill at top speed. She was very frightened indeed. Why had the toys shouted goodbye? Was it a trick they had played on her to get rid of her? Amelia Jane wailed aloud as she shot down the hill. Oh dear, oh dear, had she been so dreadful that the toys wanted to get rid of her like that?

'I'm going straight into the stream!' she squealed, and splash, into the water she went.

She clung to the tray. It didn't sink, but bobbed on the surface, with a very wet Amelia Jane clinging on top. Down the stream she went, bobbing on the waves.

She floated for a very long way. Then

the tray bumped into the bank, stuck into some weeds and stopped. Amelia thankfully crawled off on to the land. She was wet and cold and tired. She could see a dog not far off and she was frightened of him.

Where could she hide? What was that lying on the grass over there? A bicycle! It had a basket behind the saddle, and Amelia Jane staggered off to it. She squeezed into the basket, and stuffed an old bit of newspaper over herself. Now, perhaps, nobody, not even the dog, would see her.

She fell asleep and dreamed of the toys. She dreamt that they were all cross with her, and she cried in her sleep.

'Don't be cross with me. I'll be good, I'll be good.'

Then she woke up – and dear me, she was wobbling from side to side in the basket. Somebody had picked up the bicycle, mounted it, and was now riding away down the river path – with Amelia Jane tucked into the basket at the back.

Oh, dear! thought Amelia, in a panic. 'Now where am I going? I'm miles and miles away from home – and from all the toys. I wish I was back again. Wouldn't I be good if I could only get back to the nursery! But the toys wouldn't be pleased to see me at all.

They'd turn me out again.'

On she went and on. Miles and miles it seemed to Amelia Jane, and she grew cramped and cold in the basket. And then, at last, the rider stopped and jumped off.

He flung his bicycle against something, and walked off, whistling.

Amelia Jane peeped out. The bicycle was against a wall near a back door. She crawled out of the basket, and almost fell to the ground. She ran to the door. If only she could get into a house, she could hide.

In she went, and somebody jumped in surprise as the big doll ran past. Amelia tore into the hall and up the stairs. She almost fell inside a room, and stopped there, panting in fright.

And will you believe it, she was back in the

nursery again – and there were all the toys she knew, staring at her in amazement – the toy soldier, the bear, the clown, the mouse and everyone!

She had come all the way home in the basket of the bicycle belonging to one of the children! He had gone to the river that day, and then had cycled all the way back – and Amelia Jane was in his basket. What a very, very peculiar thing!

'You said goodbye to me – but here I am again,' said Amelia, in a funny, shaky sort of voice. 'It seems as if you c-c-c-can't get rid of me!'

She burst into tears – and then everyone ran to comfort her. She was patted and fussed, and even Tom kept saying he was glad to see her back.

'Oh, dear – this is all so nice,' said Amelia at last. 'I won't be mischievous again, toys. I won't play tricks any more. I'll be just as good as gold!'

'We don't believe you,' said Tom. 'But never mind – we're glad to have you back, you bad, naughty doll. We never *really* want to say goodbye to you, Amelia Jane!'

I don't either. What about you?